The L

To Mary Jo,
Best wishes!
Karen Jasper

Karen Jasper

CHIHUAHUA PRESS

NORTHAMPTON, MA

CHIHUAHUA PRESS
Northampton MA 01062

ISBN: 9780615231112

First Chihuahua Press paperback edition 2008

Manufactured in the United States of America

For information regarding readings, autographed book plates, book clubs,
and special discounts, contact the author at karenjasper@comcast.net

Dedication

"If you tame me, it will be as if the sun came to shine on my life."

The Little Prince, Antoine de Saint Exupéry

To Rose Delfino, my mother, who somehow managed the difficult feat of teaching me to be wild and tame at the same time,

To Janet Beattie, my partner in life and love for more than two decades, who has supported every single crazy thing I've attempted,

To Jessica Jasper Cochrane, my daughter, who has taught me about deep love over and over and over again,

And to Cecilia Court, my spirited and talented friend, whose colors and words will shine forever bright.

Acknowledgements

Two Octobers ago, with crunchy leaves covering her walkway, I timidly walked into Nerissa Nields' living room and the Big Yellow writing group for the first time. (Only we writers call it the Big Yellow, named after her towering egg yolk colored house. Nerissa calls the group *"Writing It Up in the Garden,"* which is more accurate since it's all about nourishing "seedlings" who love to write.) I read my work out loud for the first time that weekend, and I haven't stopped shopping for words since.

I am a Counselor by training and profession, and that has given me human connections and rich observations for most of my adult life. Currently I have clients who struggle to find themselves and others to keep the electricity on and the demons out. I am also surrounded by fellow writers and talented artists who see the world in technicolor. Sometimes my words and characters come from my imagination but most often, it's the people around me who guide me to the big ideas and nuanced observations.

This is my first novel. I've written the story of Alex and Lily with the hope that the definition of family and the simplicity of love is wide, not narrow, and is inclusive, not restrictive. I suppose the premise of two women loving one another so passionately might offend some on religious or moral grounds. Certainly the issues of honor and obligation and betrayal and self preservation are part of this story, but I hope I've gotten it all more right than wrong.

Try as I might to be more "realistic," I believe in love, and I am indebted to countless people in my life who have shared and supported and encouraged that belief every step of the way. Thank you first to my fellow Big Yellow writers: Nerissa Nields, Melissa Miller, Kris McCue, Lora Nielsen, Nichole Burton, Bill Michalski, Matthew Harvey, Tracie Potochnik, Samira Katherine Hotchkiss Mehta, Rick Adam, Ashley King, Teresa Wong, and the late and sorely missed Andrea Coller.

A special thanks to Lora Nielsen, who spent a weekend with me solely to sit in the backyard together to review and edit every line and every word of my manuscript;

To Editor Brenda Hill, whose feedback and guidance made the book stronger and better;

To Valerie Walsh, (my blog pal 'Valgal') who offered me the unbelievable gift of an original painting for the book's cover, the result of which you can magically see for yourself;

To Bill Michalski, my friend and a talented graphic designer, for his fantastic page layout, cover design and steady patience;

To my dear JB, who proofed the story of Alex and Lily at least six times;

To Ces, who can move my creative juices from first to fourth gear in ten seconds flat;

To my friends Maureen Keeley and Cheryl Greaney, who taught me about the grace and gravity of living with cancer;

To my friends Heather Heins, Marsha Stone, Jonathan Parad, and Liz Summa, who read the manuscript in its early stages and took the time to tell me how to improve it;

To my blogging buddies, many of whom have been there from the first moment my writing became public. Thank you to CS (Citizen of the World), Debra Kay (Beam Me Up Scotty), Anonymous Bird, Singleton (The Hippie Parade), Skinny (Skinny Little Sister), Melissa (Forge Light), Ces (Ces & Her Dishes), Miladysa, ValGal (The Artistic Adventures of Valerie Walsh), Kris (Nothing Would Ever Happen), Carla (Anonyrrie) Peterbie, Red Mojo (Half a Bubble Off), Kay (Made for Weather),

Menchie (Timeouts), Jessie (Diary of a Self Portrait), Ruby (The Ruby Diaries), Sidney (My Sarisari Store), Andrea (Colouring Outside the Lines), Bibi (Bibi's Beat), Lavender (The Birds and the Bees), Wieneke (Het Tweede Deel), Hildegarde (Flanders Inside), Nichole (Fumblerette), Greta Jane (Ivory Needles), Lauren, Cherry Pie (Dipping My Toes Back in the Water), Auntie Mim, Forever Young, Tammy (My Daily Warrior), Merlin Princesse, Homo Escapeons, Liz (Quiet in the Stacks), Maria (Pieces of M.E.), J- (Hopeful Notations), and Willie Baronet. If it weren't for the visits and comments of my blog-friends, I doubt I would have ever had the confidence to finish the book, let alone publish it;

To the women and men everywhere who live and sometimes die with cancer;

To members of the gay and lesbian community who have forged the path and deserve the result;

To all the different combinations and shapes of families, who despite the judgments and challenges, live their lives and share their love;

And finally, to you the reader: it means a great deal to me that you hold the story of Alex and Lily in your hands. Thank you.

Prologue

The Star

Twinkle, twinkle, little star,
How I wonder what you are !
Up above the world so high,
Like a diamond in the sky.

When the blazing sun is gone,
When he nothing shines upon,
Then you show your little light,
Twinkle, twinkle, all the night.

Then the trav'ller in the dark,
Thanks you for your tiny spark,
He could not see which way to go,
If you did not twinkle so.

In the dark blue sky you keep,
And often thro' my curtains peep,
For you never shut your eye,
Till the sun is in the sky.

'Tis your bright and tiny spark,
Lights the trav'ller in the dark :
Tho' I know not what you are,
Twinkle, twinkle, little star.

Written by the sisters
Ann & Jane Taylor, 1806

1

Never!—this hysterical exclamation hammering in her head with a high heel thump, followed by a more reasoned, *No, no, no, it's a joke.*

But there was the envelope, the kind usually reserved for international mail, with three 39 cent stamps in the right hand corner, her wide scribbly name and address dead center, and a return address that stopped her cold. Cold as in chilling. Chilling as in frozen.

When Lily was ten years old, she was hit in the face with a random soccer ball. It knocked her to the ground so fast that it took several minutes before she felt the full force of the impact. This is how she felt now, the recipient of a body slam so sudden and violent she barely had time to feel the punch.

She should have waited until she felt more in control, but instead she opened the envelope, careful not tear it or the letter inside. She pulled out four pristine pieces of white linen paper, the handwriting on each page less circular and more controlled, as though the writer was trying to reign in her thoughts by lassoing her words.

Just seeing the beloved handwriting brought tears.

"Dear Lily,

For years I've thought about this letter. I owed you an explanation you never got and I will understand if you have no interest or need for one now. But I hope you will hear me out. I have been carrying these words for seven years now, and it is only because I may die that I find the need and the courage to tell you the truth."

Lily stared at the handwriting in disbelief. Struggling to steady herself, she acted instinctively to protect the letter from getting irreparably smudged, and that reflexive act was her second surprise of the day.

2

"I couldn't do it, Lily. I saw my Mother's face telling me it was wrong, I thought about how much my husband trusted me, that Andy would hate me, my upbringing. I believed it was carnal and selfish, and the only way I could atone was to suffer. Life without you would be the greatest suffering I could ever choose, so that is what I did. Even now I know I could not have lived with myself. I did what I thought was right, and I decided it would be easier for you if I ended it badly. So many times I let you think I had responded because I loved and needed you, not because I wanted to. And those times I told you it could never ever be, I knew you wouldn't be able to truly trust me after that. Through it all I thought maybe time *would put things in perspective for us, and maybe some day we'd be friends."*

Lily's eyes widened. Her composure was melting into a waxless mess, leaving this pristine letter with the little girl circular handwriting, explaining the unexplainable, karate chopping at the knees what had taken her seven long years to rebuild. It had been ten years in all: three when they had lovingly and impossibly tried to carve a life together, three with Lily buried under pillow-over-head agony, and the last four, when life was finally good again.

Aware that her emotions were free falling, Lily recalled Alex's numerous apologies before all words stopped all together, the different spins at different times, each hurting more than the last. Now here was another penance at the worse possible time. Here was this little girl circular handwriting the week before Lily, in front of family and friends, would join with and commit to a woman named Maxine Larson, the week before the first day that would prove once and for all that Lily was finally free.

The letter continued:

"Every day for all this time, I've tried to accept what I did and understand why it had to be. It took more than a year before I stopped thinking about you constantly, and finally, over time, I settled into life with Mike and the kids. But I was no longer the same person. I didn't see things in the same way, and everything I did I would

wish and wonder what it would be like if you were there too. Every day I hoped that you found what you hoped for in me."

Lily's tenuous hold gave way to simmering anger. This was too much. *Found what I hoped for? How exactly would I do that Alex? I've had to settle too, every minute of every day. I'm sorry you're sick, but honest to God, maybe it would be easier for me to read your obituary than another apology. You should know I can't handle this, Alex.*

And yet, Lily read on.

"I got the diagnosis a few months ago. I'll spare the details but it's the big C. I've reeled and thrown dishes and grieved and prayed. I've done everything I can, including handing it over to whatever God or Goddess I wish I believed in. I've taken inventory, sorted my priorities, and rearranged my time. My sister Paula will help Mike with the kids. Andy is now 17 and Amy's 16. Remember when they used indelible magic markers on every sheet and pillow case in the house to make a Buddhist temple in the living room? It's pretty much the same madness except now it's more about cars and clothes and midnight curfews. Bottom line: In case I die, I've taken care of everything. Except us."

Hearing about the kids was too much. There was more to read but Lily couldn't focus or catch her breath.

She slid down on the couch, her cheeks burning and her eyes blurred. A throbbing headache would keep her in hiding the next day.

She remembered the last time she saw the kids. It had been a bleak damp Friday afternoon and Andy, then ten, had the role of Davy Crockett in his school play. Lily had winced at his raccoon hat, a fluffy disgusting tail of some skinned animal blowing every which way each time he moved, and Andy moved. He had forgotten his lines midway through, but in or out of character he had charmed the audience into believing the gibberish he skillfully substituted. Andy, with his wry wit and wide heart, was a good boy, a good sport, a son and brother anyone would be proud of. Lily considered him her friend and he was good at that too.

And Amy, nine going on sixteen that afternoon at the Blue Bonnet Diner, begging her mother to wear eye shadow, whining about the gross looking sweet potato fries and smothering the bright orange buds with red ketchup. Mike was working out of town as he often was on Fridays so it was Alex, their two children, and Lily, her guiding hand on Alex's elbow, gleefully dodging raindrops and defiantly waving their umbrellas, crisscrossing around puddles and marching single file through parked cars. They walked light, the kids on each side of them, laughing, teasing Andy about his improvisation, that afternoon when Lily dared to think this could last. She and Alex had known each other for three years. They had struggled and soared together, frequently talking on the phone past midnight like teenagers, often shopping and hiking and sharing errands and energy—and only occasionally putting words to feelings that simmered and sometimes erupted.

3

Three weeks after that lovely wet day, Alex called just before midnight.

"I told Mike, Lily," she said, her voice on the edge of hysteria.

Lily understood immediately.

"I had to, Lily. He pulled it out of me and I couldn't lie. I told him, yes, I love you. I told him I hoped we could figure it out but he exploded. He threw the oriental lamp against the wall and stormed out. I won't dignify what he called me. I just sat there and shook. I was afraid to call you. He came back three hours later and told me, then and there, I'd better choose. He said he would file for divorce the next day if I ever saw you again."

Lily was stunned, but not surprised. Who could blame this heterosexual woman with her designer wedding band, mother to these precious children, her sexuality and passion and love and loyalty all misfiring at the same time? Still, she couldn't believe Alex hadn't discussed this with her before she put a reality into motion that assured the obvious consequence that all hell would break loose.

"I told him I had to see you in person, Lily, I insisted on that."

"Why?" Lily had asked. She could barely speak. She struggled to breathe.

"I owe you that much." Alex paused. It was a long pause, the kind where there's enough time to watch and wait for the broken pieces to shatter as they fall.

Then she simply said, "I will miss you, Lily." These words, spoken in soft slow-motion, entered Lily's inner sanctuary and tipped and turned over and upside down an emotional frying pan, spattering the hot oil of betrayal and loss everywhere. Lily was devastated. Four words, *"I will miss you."* The die was cast, the deal was done. She had no part in a decision already made and a burden now firmly rooted, one that she understood years ago she would carry for the rest of her life.

"Let's say goodbye now, Alex," Lily had said.

There was another pause. Probably more words were spoken but Lily remembered only the last sentence.

"You can call me at work, Lily, anytime, you know."

There should have been more to say. So much had

been said already, but Lily knew it would never be enough. So many times they had tried to make sense of what was improbably and impossibly true. But not this time. This time Mike knew.

Lily held the phone to her chest until the shrill beep beep beep finally stopped. She placed the receiver, still off the hook, on the coffee table, stood and shut the living room blinds. She lay on the couch, buried under a green chenille blanket, until ten hours later, when the dogs began to whine. She opened the door to the fenced in back yard, measured out two cups of dry food for each of them, and forced herself into the shower, where she scrubbed clean, passively watching a glorious future, now erased by the present, violently swirl down the drain.

4

How does someone become a lesbian anyway? Who would choose all the baggage that comes with it: family scorn, God's wrath, periodic insecurity, and unforeseen safety concerns all in the same package?

Alex Fournier, small business owner, wife to Mike and mother to Andy and Amy, knew she would like Lily Peterson as soon as she pulled into her driveway and took note of her garden. It was late May and Alex was quick to notice the pink inpatients confidently planted in front of two large leaf sorrels-the edible kind with the vibrant green colors that went so well as a backdrop.

Hmmmm, she thought, *this woman knows what she's doing. And she has her act together a week ahead of Memorial Day-risky but clever.*

Alex followed the flower beds to a brick walkway. She approached a newly painted eggplant colored front door and knocked twice. Lily opened the door, smiled warmly, and extended her hand to Alex, who was nervously scanning the scene in search of her friend Willa. When she finally made eye contact with Lily, Alex was a bit startled by how attractive and normal she looked–tall and willowy and fashionably comfortable in her own skin.

From the moment they stood in Lily's peach colored closet of a hallway, its walls covered with dozens of framed photos, a carved coconut head from Bali, a wooden giraffe head from Toys R' Us, and several six by eight framed collages made by Lily's college age niece, Alex knew that Willa was spot on.

She was attending the Bag Ladies Book Club for the first time. Willa had clued her in on several of the attendees already: Mairead, a Web Designer who laughed easily with a charming Irish brogue and pronounced GAR-age instead of garage; Roberta, a School Psychologist whose daughter had recently become transgendered; Allison, a Nurse Case Manager who was featured in the *Boston Globe* for pulling a teen from the Charles River and saving his life with CPR; and Lily, the hostess for the evening, who happened to be a lesbian, and about whom Willa had gushed in great detail.

Where Alex was cute and solid and preppy, remnants still from her high school days as a cheerleader and second runner up Prom Queen, Lily was tall and slim and graceful. At first glance Alex dubbed her a "designer bohemian," dressed in a tie-dye shirt that dropped to just above her hips and looked perfect with her fitted jeans.

This night a group of eight women were discussing Toni Morrison's *Beloved*. Alex noticed how confidently Lily offered her opinions, how thoughtfully she listened to everyone else, and how her easy going persona seemed to energize the room. She especially liked what Lily, a college instructor in English and Ethics, had to say about responsibility and obligation. As a wife and mother, that struck a chord in Alex.

"I mean how do you know when or why you just have to put yourself first?" Alex had asked the group.

And Lily had answered, "When you're drowning, you know."

Alex could see that everyone there liked Lily. She was the kind of friend anyone would want. It wasn't as though Alex lacked friends–she had been voted Personality Plus in high school after all–but the truth was that for more than two years she had been bored with the elements of her daily life. It was difficult for her to face, but Alex was not entirely happy. She and Mike had married straight out of college, Andy was born a year later, and Amy a year after that. They played whist every Friday night with Mike's college roommate and his accountant wife, they took the kids to Disney World every other winter and rented a cottage on Cape Cod for two weeks every summer. They both cooked dinners for the family; they had sex two or three times a week; they talked and gardened together. Mike was a good father, a good husband, a good guy. She should have been quite satisfied. But she wasn't.

By the third week, unsure whether her discontent contributed to her interest in Lily, Alex considered asking her to dinner. On the fifth week, as the Bag Ladies were dispersing, she took the plunge. By then she knew Lily taught college literature, volunteered on two non-profit boards, and had twice vacationed in France. Would she be too busy, her life too full already, to consider a new friendship? Alex wasn't shy: she was a bona fide extrovert with a wicked sense of humor, but she often retreated rather than risk either embarrassment or vulnerability. This time, however, she had promised herself to push through and try. What could she lose by trying?

"Lily," Alex said, "would you have any interest in getting together sometime?"

Lily smiled. "Sure."

Alex was prepared. "Do you like fondue? What about the fondue special at Marsh's Landing? It's right on the river and it's not usually crowded."

"Sure," Lily said.

Alex was suddenly not prepared. She stuttered, "Friday night? At six?"

"Sure," Lily said.

Alex smiled. So did Lily.

5

In high school Alex began phoning a fellow cheerleader named Carolyn Jenkins. Carolyn responded cordially but it became pretty clear pretty quickly that she was too into her football captain boyfriend to expand her social circle to include a new friend. Alex didn't think much about it at the time, but on the drive back from Lily's, she thought about Carolyn Jenkins.

6

Five weeks after their first meeting, Lily pulled her Mazda into Alex's driveway just as a little girl and her two wheel bike approached. Lily opened her car door and greeted the child, who stood around 4 foot 3 inches and was dressed in a 'My Little Pony' tee shirt and jeans with ironed creases and folded cuffs. Her brown curly hair fell just below her ears. She stared at Lily and smiled.

"Hello," Lily said. "My name is Lily. I'm here to see your mother, I think."

Amy stared at her. "Are you her new friend from Bag Ladies?"

"Yes," Lily smiled. "From the book club."

"I'll tell her you're here," Amy said, "or do you want

to come in? That would be okay if you want to." But before Lily could answer, Amy had kicked her bike stand in place and scooted toward the front door.

Lily stood in the driveway and looked at the three story grey Queen Ann Victorian with pink trim. She estimated it sat on a third of an acre or so, enough land to extend Alex's landscaping project well beyond her ambitious timetable. The neighborhood was lined with mature maple trees on both sides of the streets, creating a dell-like canopy. It felt secure and safe, and Lily liked that Alex lived here.

The front door swung open and Lily turned to see Alex approaching, holding Amy's hand and awkwardly waving. Aware of her own jumpiness, she could tell that Alex was nervous, and that brought her some relief.

Lily responded warmly when Alex greeted her with a firm hug and smile, then still holding Amy's hand, she said, "Lily, may I introduce you to my favorite daughter?"

Amy squinted. "Mom, I'm your only daughter. Besides, we already met. From Bag Ladies, right?" she said confidently, as if she had just aced her 4th grade history quiz.

Alex leaned down and kissed Amy on the top of her head. "Bath and bedtime by 8:30, honey. Don't give your father a hard time."

"When will you be home, Mom?" Amy asked.

A certain shyness washed over Alex's face and Lily saw it. She looked indecisively at Lily and then back to

Amy. "Probably after you're asleep, but I'll come in and kiss you goodnight."

Amy extended her hand to Lily. "Nice to meet you, Miss Lily Bag Lady."

Lily took her hand and bowed. "And nice to meet you, Ms. Amy Fournier."

7

For months after the finality of their last phone call and final goodbye, Lily processed the conversation in her head so often she regularly fell asleep recalling it word for word. Alex would be gone. Mike knew and Alex would be gone. That's all there was to it. Of course Lily had prepared for this outcome a hundred times or more, but not entirely. She operated on a parallel reality where she and Alex would find an honorable way to stay together and prosper. She allowed herself to believe this by periodically reviewing the facts. After all, they never went even a day without connecting and catching up, never more than a few days without finding a way to see each other, never a week without somehow confirming the obvious trust and fire that simmered between them.

But this time reality could not be altered. It was over. It needed to be over. Lily would make sure that the outcome Alex desired was put forth and kept in place.

She would clamp shut the love that was Alex and Lily and make it so air tight there would be no way they could come up for air and no choice but to hope that years later they would both re-emerge in some semblance of whole.

That is what Lily had done for seven years, until one Saturday morning at 11:32 am, when she held a letter from Alex Louise Fournier in her reluctant shaking hands.

8

From the moment Lily opened the car door for her, Alex was surprised how date-like this all felt. They had met each other just five weeks ago, seen each other just five times in their book club, and now here they were heading to Marsh's Landing together. Though she tried to direct her vision elsewhere, Alex couldn't take her eyes off Lily. She stared at the graceful way she moved her hands, and she noticed her earnest gaze when they made eye contact. *Was this a date?* Alex wondered. For a moment, she panicked. *Ohmygod, what if she thinks I'm coming on to her?*

"So how many times have you been to Europe?" she asked two minutes into their fifteen minute drive.

"Three," Lily said. "Twice to France and once to Italy."

"What was your favorite?"

Lily didn't hesitate. "Paris. Paris is my favorite of anywhere. Have you been there?"

"No," Alex said, "but it's on my list."

"The next time I take my students there, maybe you might want to come along. We're always looking for level headed chaperones." Lily outwardly smiled and Alex inwardly melted.

"Fat chance of that happening. I have these two little ones at home who block the door when I try to get away without them. I have to work on them for weeks before my spa weekend with my sister. Did you notice how Amy made sure she checked you out?" Alex threw her head back and laughed. "She's a little mother sometimes."

"I have a niece about her age," Lily said.

"Have you ever been married, Lily? Or committed, I guess I mean?" Alex asked.

Thrown by the sudden change of subject, Lily paused. "Well, I was in a relationship with a woman named Julie for four years. We broke up because I couldn't compete with her passion for her work, but we still keep in touch every once in a while."

"Who left who?" Alex asked.

"I left her, but she kind of checked out long before that."

"Did you love her?"

"Yes, I did. She's a painter and I loved how she saw the world in such a vibrant way. Taking a walk with her was like visiting a museum. She noticed the sway of the grass and turn of the leaves and the way the light bounced off the lake. She is a good person and an incredible talent, but her art kept pulling her away. We'd have wonderful intimate days and nights and weeks and then, she'd be gone. I couldn't get used to that–probably all my abandonment issues." Lily laughed. "What about you?"

"I've been with Mike since college. We got married and had kids. We both work full time. He's a good guy and an excellent father." Alex paused as if her words had dried up. She stared at her hands, twisting a Kleenex in her lap, until Lily interrupted the awkward silence.

"Congratulations on the longevity of your marriage. That's quite an achievement, all that time."

Her face flushed, Alex turned to her. "It's tough, actually. Sometimes I don't know if I'm happy or not. I love the guy, don't get me wrong, but it's just kind of boring. We still have sex probably three times a week, but day to day, it's all too rote and too predictable. I've never told him, but sometimes I think I'd be better off by myself. And maybe him too."

Lily pulled the Mazda into the parking lot and looked at Alex, who was holding back obvious emotion. "Is that why you asked that question in Bag Ladies about putting yourself first?" she asked.

Alex responded, "Yeah…but hey, I don't want you to get the wrong impression. I'm not someone who just bitches about things."

Lily looked at her tenderly. "I know that."

Alex added, "And I'd like to get to know you not because of what I just told you."

Lily felt a strange warmth inside her. She looked directly at Alex and half smiled.

"Alex, I'm glad to get to know you. I love your honesty."

Alex snickered, "You mean my raw screwed up vulnerability?"

Lily half laughed. "Yeah, that's what I mean."

9

With less than two feet between them they walked into the restaurant and sat across from each other at a square table in front of an oversized window overlooking the Connecticut River. They each ordered a glass of Pinot Grigio and awkwardly stared at the menu until Lily asked Alex about her work.

"Well, I own my own company, a consulting firm specializing in website design. Don't ask me how I got into this work or how I've been successful for that matter. I'm good at design but not at programming, but somehow we landed a contract with the state and we've kept growing."

Lily grinned. "So you're a big cheese business woman."

"Ha!" said Alex, "More like a little sandwich, but I'm proud of myself for getting this far. I have eight employees and it's mostly fun."

"You seem to have it pretty much together, Alex."

"Hardly. I'm as lost as a woman can be right now. I show up, I do do that, but I want life to be a Cadillac and it feels like a Chevy."

Lily looked at Alex. The change in her expression and body language was jarring. She wanted to be supportive but not intrusive.

"What you said in the car about being bored: I know what you mean. When Julie moved out, it was a relief. Better to have a good relationship just with yourself if that's the best you can do. But you have kids. You've got a few years ahead before you'll be footloose. And it sounds like all in all you love your husband."

"Oh God," Alex said, "you can't help but love Mike. He's really a good guy most of the time. It's the passion that's missing. Sometimes he feels like my brother. I often wonder if he feels the same way. Still, I'm not a fan of divorce. We love our kids and wouldn't hurt them for anything. They have the most wondrous way of keeping things real. Do you like kids, Lily?"

Lily didn't hesitate. "I love them."

"Hey, do you want to come bowling with us some Saturday?"

"Sure," Lily said.

"That's what you said when I asked you if you'd like to get together."

"What?"

"Sure."

"Sure what?" Lily turned her head in a way Alex would come to adore.

Alex laughed. "When I asked you to dinner, you just said 'sure'. Is that what you always say?"

Lily smiled. "No Alex. I hardly ever say sure."

"Oh, well then," Alex replied.

Lily noticed the same certain shyness on her new friend's face.

They laughed when their fondue forks got tangled up and they ended the evening with a shared piece of chocolate mud cake and two steamed cappuccinos. By the time they walked out of Marsh's Landing, they were talking like the old souls they would become, telling stories about their respective teenage years, transitions to adulthood, and the emotional limitations of men.

"Boy, you're fun to talk to, Lily. I feel like I've known you forever."

Lily saw that shyness once again. She smiled. "Well, Willa said we'd like each other. Should we do this again?"

Alex didn't hesitate. "How about next Friday? A movie maybe?"

Lily grinned. "Sure," she said.

And with that exchange, the saga of Lily and Alex took root. The Mazda pulled up to Alex's house at 10:05 pm and Alex put her hand on Lily's shoulder.

"This was really nice, Lily. Thanks for making time for me."

"Sure," Lily said.

"See, you said it again!"

"What?"

"Sure."

"Well, it is sure."

"Good. I'm glad," Alex said.

"Okay."

"Great."

Alex leaned across the auto console and hugged Lily. Afterwards, Lily was not certain but it seemed to her that they had both been reluctant to say goodnight. The length of her drive home, she kept reviewing the evening, aware that she was smiling. *She's adorable. I love how she just puts it out there. Did I read her right? Did she seem interested in me? Holey Moley.*

And fifteen miles back, in the master bedroom of a pink and grey Victorian on a street lined with maple trees, Alex Louise Fournier was asking herself a similar version of the same questions.

10

"I expected it to be hard at first," the letter continued, "Every thing I did reminded me of you. I would put the Trader Joe's can of fried onion rings in my cart and think, Oh, Lily loves these. Remember when we forgot the green bean casserole in the oven and the smoke got so thick it took us two hours to clear the house out? Or I would see someone wearing a fake leopard coat and I would imagine you strutting across the room, looking like Rita Moreno with your knee high black boots and that chenille blue scarf I love. I expected a period of horrible pain. I was prepared for it. I focused on Andy and Amy. When I saw Mike trying so hard to be more attentive and thought-ful to me, I tried to settle in with him, like it was before

I met you. I tried. For months. And then years. I wasn't surprised when you didn't respond to my Christmas card. Or to my phone message. I figured out you needed me to keep away, to be sure I did not hurt you all over again.

"*But Lily, it never did get better.*

"*I went to a psychic after I got my diagnosis. I was desperate to hear that I would live, Lily, that this damn cancer would not take me out. Instead, she talked about us. She said that you and I are soul mates. That's the first thing she said—that no matter what we did or didn't do, we could never be happy without each other. Here I'm wanting reassurances that I won't die and I walked out of there oddly relieved just thinking about you. I know what you're thinking: I'm as utopic as ever. But really, how could any normal person think otherwise: how would she have even known about you?*"

Lily put the letter down. She sat upright, remembering how hard she worked at her posture in parochial school after Sister Agnes told her she would spend time in purgatory if she did not sit properly at Mass. She sat properly now, perfectly aligned in the service of the Lord, waiting for the start of the organ pipes and the blessing of the Sacrament to tell her what the holy hell she should be feeling.

11

Lily bought the tickets and Alex bought the popcorn. With the theatre only half full, they chose two middle seats in an empty row midway from the screen. When they sat down and settled in, their arms touched each other's down to their elbows and neither of them moved to alter that. Midway through Lily reached for Alex's hand and neither of them moved to alter that either. When they got up to leave, Lily guided Alex though the darkened theatre and into the eye squinting lobby. Neither said a word, but when they got in the car, they looked at each other and smiled.

"How about coffee at Esselon?" Lily asked.

"Super," Alex said.

The Esselon Café was a wide open place with a high tin ceiling and a huge coffee bean machine tucked in a back corner. They chose a two top table nestled by a corner window, and ordered two cappuccinos.

"Where's your favorite place in the world, Alex?" Lily asked.

"I love water," Alex said. "My husband and I take the kids to Cape Cod almost every summer. If I didn't have to work, I would want to be at a beach house on the outer cape. Maybe Truro or Eastham. Possibly P-town if I could have a little patch of land with it."

Lily nodded. "I go to Provincetown every summer for a couple of weeks. I've gotten in the habit of writing and working on my books there, so I give myself the luxury of renting a second floor waterfront place in the East End. I try to get a one bedroom but if it's just a one room studio, that's fine with me."

"Are most of your friends lesbian?" The question jumped out of Alex's mouth before her censor could pull it back. Startled, Lily smiled.

"No, not at all. But I certainly have friends and colleagues who are gay and lesbian. And some who are heterosexually single, or married, or divorced, and I have one colleague who is bisexual. And a nephew who became my niece three years ago. But my best friend Wendy is straight. In fact she's still actively searching for her version of Mr. Right. I keep telling her nobody's perfect, but she's not giving up." Lily looked up. "Are lesbians unfamiliar to you, Alex?" she asked.

"No, and I'm not uncomfortable either," Alex replied. "But for some reason I'm a little nervous around you."

Lily almost said, *'Is it because I'm attracted to you?'* but quickly thought the better of it. Instead, she nodded, "Well, I'm a little nervous with you too. I think it's because you're so honest talking about yourself. It makes it easier for me to be myself."

A light switch turned on for Alex and it showed on her face. "That's it! I've wondered why I feel so relaxed with you," she said. "That's how I feel with you too. It's so easy to be myself."

Their ease together became Friday Girls Night Out, then some wild afternoons of candlepin bowling with the Fournier kids. Lily got in the habit of kissing Alex on the side of her neck whenever they embraced, which they always did during greetings and farewells. She knew she was allowing her feelings to outpace their friendship, she had no idea what any of this might mean to Alex, and they were not discussing it. Instead they focused on their considerable good fortune.

"You could be my best friend, Lily," Alex announced one evening over mussels. "That comes with certain responsibilities."

"Really?" Lily teased, "Like what?"

"Well, you have to love me no matter what."

"Okay," Lily said. "What else?"

"You have to laugh at all my jokes."

"Fine. What else?"

"You have to be patient with me."

Lily almost asked for a clarification that was unnecessary. Instead, she looked at Alex and said, "Sure I will."

"Me too," Alex said. "That is, if I could be your best friend too."

Lily grinned. "Sure Alex," she said. "Even double sure."

12

They had known each other sixteen months when they went to Paris. By then Lily and Alex routinely saw each other every Wednesday night at their weekly Book Club meetings and most Saturday afternoons over lunch during Amy's dance lessons. And sometimes, with both Amy and Andy in tow, the afternoon would extend to a matinee movie or a local art exhibit, or to Lily's goofy amazement, multiple strings of candlepin bowling. The kids loved to bowl and were happily oblivious to the sad fact that not one of the four of them ever once broke a hundred.

"Lily," Alex had said, "Your bowling sucks."

"Alex," Lily replied, "I wouldn't talk about my bowling if I were you. You just about crack the alley when you throw the ball."

"Yes, but Lily, you look like an ostrich when you throw the ball. That's worse."

Lily chuckled. "Not if you're the owner of the bowling alley, it's not."

Except for a spa weekend with her sister Paula every other weary February and her every-other-year summer trip with her college buddies, Alex could not recall a vacation without Mike and the kids. She had struggled for weeks about whether to go. By the time she told Lily she was in, Alex knew she might be stepping deeper and further into a whirlpool of emotions that she had thus far, with mixed results, wrestled to control.

Lily was in charge of their tickets and passports. She carried them in a worn camel colored leather pouch she had picked up in Milan a few years ago while supervising a student exchange program. Although she was not superstitious, she used the pouch only for special occasions. This would be the first time she and Alex would travel together, that they would spend extended time together. Twice when Mike was out of town Lily had occupied the Fournier guest bedroom for the weekend, but a week in Paris–this was something along the lines of the impossible and improbable, and they both knew it.

Lily had been eyeing the eight day self guided Paris tour through the Show-of-the-Month Travel Club for several months. One Saturday, over scallops and risotto at the Daily Catch, she casually asked Alex if she had either the interest or inclination to go.

Alex listened to the itinerary and cost and simply replied, "Maybe."

When several weeks passed without further mention of the trip, Lily was surprised, as bowling balls flew, to hear an uncharacteristic total nonchalance in Alex's voice.

"I checked with Mike," she said. "I can make that Paris trip with you."

Lily, who was not prone to hyperbole and had herself mastered the art of understatement, smoothly responded.

"Great," she said, "I'll book it."

That night, as Lily lay in her bed, with a full moon casting a perfect spotlight on the apple green walls of her bedroom, she acknowledged a desire that she had not allowed herself to feel. She and Alex would be together for eight days and seven nights. Though in the preceding months they publicly walked with their arms around or tucked into one another, and Lily felt a warm rush when Alex called her 'honey girl', Lily had managed to control her thinking. She never failed to ask for guidance in her nightly prayers, and she'd never allowed her thoughts to wander too far. Until now.

On this night she did not bother to affirm her honor, or to find comfort in the solid and safe life she had built for herself. Instead, she saw herself standing beside Alex, their hands joined and their arms playfully swinging in unison, secure and anchored to each other. This was the image Lily thought about for the minutes just before she fell asleep, soon to dream that she was inside Dar Williams' folksong wandering the hills of Iowa, gruesomely searching for the love of her life.

13

Lily walked to the kitchen, put on the kettle and prepared a cup of hot tea, wrapping her fingers around the warm rim of the cup as if to garner protection. She walked back to the couch, sat down with the overstuffed purple satin pillow behind her, and continued reading:

"You know what a pro I am in burying emotions I refuse to face. But when I started feeling really sick, I needed you. I'd go for tests and chemo and Mike and I would sit down with the doctors and I just kept thinking 'I need Lily'.

"I broke down when Dr. Chambliss told me I was definitely stage 3. That's one step away from packing it

in. Mike and I went to the Easy Street Diner, remember that place? It's where we couldn't stop laughing when you dropped your nachos and they splattered all over that nerdy guy's new shoes, the ones with those gross little tassels on them? Anyway, Mike was as shell-shocked as I was but he tried to comfort me, he really tried. I put my face in my hands and all I could say was, 'Mike, I need to call Lily'. He looked at me and said 'Jesus Alex'. He dropped me home without another word and came back a few hours later. He looked worse than when we first heard my diagnosis. He didn't say anything about it for days. We'd make small talk at dinner and go to Andy's games together, but I could see he was trying to protect himself. I wanted to reassure him, to help him be safe, but I couldn't.

Finally, one night when the kids were out, he asked me to sit down, he told me that he loved me, that I was an asshole making the biggest mistake of my life, but I should stop trying. He cried, Lily. He told me he would stay with me if I wanted that, help me through my treatments, work out something fair with the kids, give me a divorce, he told me he would let me go, that he knew I am not a bad person. We cried together, Lily, and I loved him then and there like he's deserved all these years."

14

If the sun were any hotter, Alex would have fainted. Rolling play dough into mermaids and fairies in the back yard, Amy looked up at her.

"Mommy, why doesn't Daddy like Lily anymore?"

"Why do you ask that, honey?"

"He called her a bitch, Mommy. I heard him."

"It's complicated, sweetie. Daddy and Lily are both good people."

"Then why did Daddy say that?"

"Mommy hurt Daddy's feelings."

"Then why didn't he call you a bitch?"

"Because he has to live with me, honey." Alex paused. "And because he loves me."

"Doesn't Daddy love Lily?"

"Not as much as I do."

"Is Lily still your friend, Mommy?"

"Yes, Amy, Lily will always be my friend."

"Then why don't you play with her anymore?"

"Sometimes things don't work out the way you want them to, honey."

"You mean Daddy could tell me to stop playing with Rachel?"

"No, Amy, this only involves adults. I'll explain when you're sixteen."

"Maybe by then you'll be friends with Lily again, Mommy." Amy put her arms around her mother's neck and squeezed her little fingers together as tightly as she could. "Don't cry, Mommy. Maybe Lily and Daddy will make up and then Lily can come bowling with us on Saturday."

15

Alex sent Lily a Christmas card seven months to the day after their last phone call. The card had two women in fake fur white coats and hats holding hands, with a caption, *'BRRRR, I'd be out in the cold without a friend like you'*. Inside Alex had written, *'Don't forget me Lily. I'd love to hear from you.'*

Lily had put the card at the bottom of her sock and underwear drawer, safe from harm and sufficiently accessible that she could easily retrieve it. Sometimes she would pull it out and run her finger along the outside of the envelope, and sometimes she would bring the card to her face, seeking Alex's familiar scent.

Sandwiched in between the last call and that card, Lily had reluctantly taken six weeks of disability leave from the college. She saw a therapist twice a week, joined a new book club, took her graduate students on a ski trip to Switzerland, adopted another dog, lost twenty pounds, began writing her book on ethics again, arranged play-times with her three year old niece Amanda, and remodeled the back porch of her sweet one level six room ranch house on Tupelo Road.

She did all this earnestly and compulsively, some mornings dragging herself from bed without a thought to what would come next and others relying on Zoloft to get herself to campus to teach her English Lit class. She forced herself to the gym several times a week and accepted the concerned protection and social invitations her friends and colleagues regularly provided. But nothing changed the hovering reality that first thing every morning and last thing every night she longed for Alex. Sometimes she would imagine her at the foot of her bed, the cocky turn of her head and her arms crossed in that ridiculous Ms. Yogi pose, reaching out for Lily, smiling, that tender wicked smile. She missed the way Alex made her feel. She missed every single everything.

Lily wondered how she became so pitiful. There were moments when the thought of the two of them together simply took over, wrapped itself around her legs and held her in place, firmly implanted on a ground of piecemeal mush and misery. She hated those moments: she might be in the back yard grilling burgers, or in her office grading papers, or walking Louie around the river, when a sound, a song, the movement of someone's hands, even the flicker of the light bulb, would carry her back to her life with Alex.

But what Lily hated most was the relentless hole in her stomach. At first she thought it was an ulcer, or a tumor, perhaps some weird stomach disorder. When it persisted beyond the medical assurance that she was healthy, she came to understand that this was the scarlet letter of a broken heart.

"Oh God," her friend Wendy had said, "it took me three years to lose that feeling after Doug left me. You can't really eat when your stomach feels that way."

"Three years?" Lily moaned. "Three years?"

"Sometimes," Wendy's voice dropped to a protective whisper. "Lily, you'll survive. You'll love again. I know you will. She really did a number on you."

"It's ridiculous," Lily responded. "I'm mourning what I hoped for, not even what I ever really had. I can't seem to keep my footing, Wendy, no matter what I do or don't do. If this is love…" Lily's eyes filled and glistened like broken glass.

"I know," Wendy said, "I know."

16

They had been together about a year when they both understood that "I love you" meant more than "I love you friend." Lily welcomed their intimacy with graceful ease, but Alex fluctuated from comfortable and content to distant and distraught. She was all over the place. Still, that didn't stop her from being playful and provocative.

"Lily," she said over fried clams and French fries one September afternoon when the tease of early fall lulled them both, "if I fell in love with someone else, would you still be my best friend?"

Lily shook her head in mock irritation. "Alex, you ask unfathomable questions."

"Well, would you?"

"I have no idea."

"Well, what do you think?"

"Alex, I think you should just love me."

Alex curled her lip. "Maybe," she smiled.

Although Alex never quite adjusted to her guilt-ridden illicit juggle, that didn't stop her from talking about their future together and regularly reminding Lily of their status as bona fide soul mates. For her part, most of the time Lily just quietly listened, nodded, smiled. She knew their feelings for one another were deep and mutual, and for Alex's sake, she thought it best to let that fact simmer on low heat. She had reluctantly come to understand that Alex did not fare well when their intimacy sizzled. And Alex was not beyond blaming Lily when they got carried away.

"That was totally your fault," she would say. "There I was innocently drinking my Chablis, grateful to have you as a friend, and you seduced me."

Lily would smile.

In various incarnations, this exchange essentially became routine: Alex surrounding herself first by false innocence and then by Lily's willing complicity.

"It's not the way it really is," Lily told Wendy, "but it's something I can do for her."

What Lily understood and kept below the surface was that Alex was compelled at certain points to issue a warning to both of them: *we can't get too comfortable, honey girl, because I can't do this.*

Every so often Lily wondered how their unorthodox union would play itself out, even though she knew the answer as clearly as she knew her own breath.

17

Lily studied the handwriting in front of her and continued reading:

"After Mike gave me benediction, that's what he did, Lily, I was a basket case for weeks. I prayed the kids didn't notice. I just kept thinking what should I do? Do I dare call Lily? Tell the kids? Move to the other bedroom?

I was too sick to go to church, which is a laugh since I hadn't gone in the two years before and haven't gone since. I thought about calling that therapist you and I saw together. Remember her? Lucille, I think her name was, with those long eyelashes and that hot pink lip liner. Remember we dubbed her Dolly Parton's sister and never went back? She told us to meditate and the path would be there. We meditated ourselves right into trouble that weekend, another of so many times that were so wonderful and so painful for us both. I've come to know how hard my guilt and ambivalence must have been for you, Lily. I wish I could have reconciled all the judgments and labels within my head, rightly organized them all and let myself love you, but I couldn't. I created a rock and a hard place for myself and everyone else I loved and I couldn't handle it. Maybe it seemed like I just wouldn't, but I really don't think I could then. It was all too confusing for me. I've spent the years since knowing that some of the happiest moments in my life have been doing nothing with you, and I've wondered a million times if I, or anyone else in my circumstance, has the right to choose that kind of nothing happiness above all else.

Sometimes after this horrid chemo, when I can't settle down or eat or sleep or outpace the pain, I concentrate on our weekend in Provincetown when the car died, you lost your wallet, our reservation got screwed up, my steak was overcooked, the whale watch was a bust—hell, even my martini was too weak and yet we laughed our way through every moment of it. I can still laugh whenever I think of that, and I wonder if the tears rolling down my cheeks are because of the chemo or because of that fantastic memory."

18

Mike walked into Hough's Tavern with his shoulders slumped and his head tight to his chest. He took small limp steps toward the bar and put both hands on the stool to steady himself before he sat down and looked up at Danny. His soft blue eyes were deep and red and hollow.

"My wife's a fucking lesbian, Danny."

Danny opened his mouth full circle, then fell back with a confused squint.

"What kind of a fucking lesbian?" He paused. "You mean like a real one?"

"Yeah," Mike said, "a real one."

"Whoa," Danny said, "you'd better see a priest, Mike. Or a marriage counselor."

Mike shook his head. "It's too late Danny. You know she's sick. She could die. Not for sure, but maybe. Her time is at a premium. Besides…" His voice trailed off.

Danny's eyes scrunched so they were almost shut. "Well what the fuck does she want if she's dying, Mike? Who the fuck would even date her?" He paused again. "That's if lesbians date, you know…"

"Remember her friend, Lily? She loves her. I've known for years. I guess she loves me too, but she loves her more. She's tried. She really has. So how can I expect..?"

Mike stopped. He sat perfectly still.

"Oh Jesus the fuck, man," Danny said. "What a bear."

"Yeah," said Mike. "What a fucking bear."

19

Lily muddled her way through three miserable unbearable Christmases, two lonely mediocre ones, and finally one surprisingly festive holiday season, courtesy of a terrific woman named Max.

Lily and Max met in a playpen. They lived on opposite ends of a three mile area replete with three colleges, moon child hippies, brilliant scholars, and one dog park. In addition to frolicking with every pedigree and mutt imaginable, they found themselves in the same spot at the same time every Saturday, and after three months of that, they fell into the routine of offering up tidbits of their lives, trading restaurant reviews, and dissecting the weekly results of *American Idol* and *Lost*.

By the time Max asked Lily to dinner, they knew the significant details of each other's relatives, the character flaws that grated at them the most, and, alas, their histories of heartbreak.

"Hey," Max blurted out during a light rain, "are you free tonight? How about meeting me for dinner?" The invitation was as relaxed as their relationship would become. Nothing complicated. Just what Lily needed.

They went to the Imperial Palace and shared a Pu-Pu platter, scallion pancakes, and one order of Pad Thai, all sandwiched in between two carafes of sake. Two weeks later they kissed on the lips. The event was not long or deep, but it was sufficiently tender that Lily thought about it for several days afterwards.

"I like her," she told Wendy. "She has a full life already. She likes dogs. She reminds me of Meryl Streep. She's smart. She's kind."

Wendy smiled. "You like her how, Lily?"

Lily smiled back. "Well," she said, "if she's not the full orchestra, she's at least the string section." Lily laughed at her own description. When she and Max had kissed, she had been strangely comforted by the soft irregular lines of her lips. Like a cello string, she thought.

They made love three weeks after their first Pu Pu platter. This was the first time that Lily had been truly aroused either physically or emotionally since Alex, and she pushed herself to be open to Max. They began spending weekends together, then planning vacations, plotting a vegetable garden in Lily's back yard, and regularly sharing a Sunday morning routine that featured honeydew melon, chicken sausages and scrambled eggs. It was during one of their Sunday mornings that Lily distantly and distinctly recognized the foreign feeling of rising hope.

"Max," Lily said, "are you sure you want me? I'm a mess, you know."

Max smiled. "I'm a mess too, Lily. Look at it this way: at least we'll have plenty of sympathy for one another."

Now, months later, with Alex's letter in front of her, Lily knew she could not go through with their commitment to each other, and especially the extravagant celebration they had planned. In a confused concoction of anger and frustration, she slammed Alex's letter onto the table and she stared into the morning air. *I'm just upset,* she told herself. *I'll take a bath and then a nap. And when I wake up I'll be okay again. I can't put my life on hold for you again, Alex. I can't. Really I can't.*

But Lily wasn't okay. And it didn't turn out the way she hoped.

20

Sometimes when you think a decision's before you, you find to your surprise it's already behind you. That's what happened to Lily after Alex's letter arrived.

"Max," she said, "I have to see you. Right away."

Max walked in holding two Dunkin Donut grande lattes and said nothing. She sat down at the kitchen table, opened the sugar packets for both of them, and waited. She did not flinch when Lily told her.

"I've never stopped loving her, Max...I've never hidden that. But I thought–I truly thought–it was over. I was okay again. I thought loving you so much would take care of it all. I never expected to hear from her again, and I never expected to fall apart when I did. She's sick,

Max. You don't deserve this, but I have to sort this out. I can't.... I can't. I..."

Lily's words were barely audible. Breathless, she felt her lungs collapsing in horrible defeat. Max opened her arms and wrapped them around Lily, and placed her head on her breast, slightly rocking her. They sat there for what seemed like hours, until Lily looked up and into Max's eyes, facing the terrible reality that the drama of her broken heart would now break another.

Not a twinge of judgment or anger creased Max's face. She smiled one of her half-smiles and stood up.

"Lily, figure it out," she said. "I'll take care of the cancellations. Please don't call me until you've figured it out. Give me that much."

With that, Max leaned down and patted Louie and Sadie, picked up her coat and placed it over her arm, kissed Lily on the top of her head, and walked out, closing the door quietly behind her.

21

"After I got my diagnosis I would look at Andy and Amy and I couldn't bear to think about them without me. And Mike. How would he manage? And my business. Who would run it? It's amazing how you take these things for granted until you've got limited time staring you in the face.

In the days that followed chemo I would lie in bed and think about what to do. Every hair on my body fell out and I was so sick. I would vomit in the little plastic wastebasket you gave me. Do you remember it? The one with the leopard design? I would listen to my private symphony of fear and helplessness, over and over and over. And Lily, I'd see your face. Your green worried *eyes and that expression you make only in dire moments. Your voice, you fluffing my pillows and nervously telling me to breathe. Breathe? I'm lying in my real bed, sick as a dog wondering if I will die, and I'm hearing your imaginary voice telling me matter-of-factly to take a yoga class. Sometimes I would laugh out loud, Lily. The rollercoaster that will always be you and me. How deep and real it is, then and now, even in my pathetic misery. Always in my dreams.*

I've struggled with this for weeks. I have a long and uncertain road ahead. I've talked to Mike, and I've prayed hard and deep. So now I just have to tell you.

I'm still here, Lily."

22

The first woman Lily ever kissed was her best friend, Gail. They were juniors in college and driving home from a Budweiser-laced frat party, crunched up in Lily's two seat yellow and white Metropolitan. Both were quite drunk and a reasonable person would have questioned Lily's ability to drive, but it was 1983, and she was more concerned with having fun than worrying about the dangers of drinking and driving.

Lily saw the red light at the last moment. She thumped to a stop at the corner of Upton and Cardinal and with an unceremonious lack of grace she and Gail landed on top of each other. Before she knew it Gail was kissing her and not just a peck.

"Whoa," Lily said, "Gail, I had no idea." She tossed her head back and laughed.

"I had no idea either," Gail slurred, chuckling with obvious satisfaction before she kissed Lily again. This time her tongue slid into and lingered in Lily's mouth, and Lily panicked and pulled away.

"Hey!" Lily said, enjoying her own chuckle. "We're at a streetlight. We could get arrested for making out and obstructing traffic." She laughed again, her words spilling one on top of one another. "Not to mention two women kissing each other. Do you get arrested for that?"

"No, Lily, you get aROUSE–sed!" At that, they laughed so hard Lily was forced to pull over, and there they and the little yellow and white Metropolitan sat, motionless for the next thirty minutes. Lily reached for Gail's hand and held it until Gail remembered her new boyfriend was waiting for her at the apartment.

Lily and Gail never kissed again and Gail went on to marry a Harvard graduate who later served as an Undersecretary in the Clinton administration.

Lily, on the other hand, dated men for another year or so before she reluctantly faced the fact that Gail's kiss was the best of all. Shortly after she graduated from Northeastern, and just before she started grad school, she answered a personal ad in the *Boston Phoenix*.

Woman seeks woman, it read. *25 year old attractive humorous professional seeks tall bright and also humor-*

ous first date, preferably over dinner and definitely including dancing at midnight.

Lily responded with a one page two paragraph letter in her best handwriting. She noted that she was a bit of an introvert, well groomed and fashionable, five foot seven inches, an aspiring English Lit professor partial to both dinner and dancing, and, she added as an afterthought, *New to Women*. At the advice of her friend Wendy, who had limited success dating two men through this method, she included a picture of herself and her phone number. Always level headed, she did not include her last name, and instead simply ended with *Sincerely, Lily*.

A woman named Lorraine called three days later, at 9:30 on a Wednesday night. They agreed to meet on Friday at Grendel's Den in Cambridge for drinks and dinner. Lorraine said she knew a lesbian bar that was clean, packed, and nearby, and she asked Lily how she felt about sex on a first date.

"Not good," Lily had said.

"That's okay," Lorraine responded. "Let's see what happens–if we're even attracted to one another."

"What happens if we're not attracted to one another?" Lily asked.

"Well then, we'll still go to the bar but maybe we'll prowl on our own."

When she hung up the phone, Lily was amused. *Is this really how it works?* she wondered. She couldn't imagine a guy ever being so blunt so fast. And yet, practically speaking, Lorraine's approach made some sense. She liked the idea of a back door, and it seemed an easy way for her to foray into her first lesbian bar. *Lorraine,* she thought, *if you're missing teeth or wearing a bowling shirt, I'll definitely be prowling elsewhere.*

23

When Alex was twelve, her parents took her to the Cambridge Esplanade where the Boston Pops and 200,000 people celebrated the nation's 200th birthday. She and her family spread three blankets together ten yards from the bank of the Charles River, where they snacked on Cokes and sausage and pepper subs and pink cotton candy while the Pops played the *1812 Overture*. With hundreds of excited festive voices all round them, they waited for the arrival of dusk. When the sky was finally black, the distant barge began firing.

This was the first time Alex saw fireworks, and these fireworks, planned and executed by a world renowned European pyrotechnic specialist, were utterly spectacular.

For thirty continuous minutes, high overhead, creating a universe of elaborately designed patterns and circles and arrows soaring upward with impeccably executed timing, a canopy of bangs and pops and rockets unleashed massive pulsating colors. Whites and greens and reds and yellows and a few precious blues, shooting up and exploding, all at once, in every corner of the sky.

When it was over, as they walked back to the Arlington Street T stop, Alex scrunched her face and pulled at her mother's arm.

"Mom," she said, "why did it feel like it would have been okay if we had all died while those fireworks were going off?"

Her mother, startled, surprised, stopped and turned to face Alex.

"Honey, some moments are like that. Some people say they feel that way in church, or when they feel really close to some one they love. You know in every bone in your body that everything is totally perfect."

Before Alex could respond, her mother added, "And honey, when you are lucky enough to have moments like that, you hold on to them as long as you can and you let them change you. Because they are gifts straight from God."

Twenty one years later, in a sparse room in Paris on the left side of two shaky pushed together twin beds, Alex understood the earnest look on her mother's face that night.

24

Alex was constant in her ambivalence. She was married with young children, Catholic, earnest, and if these reasons were not enough, she worried about her reputation. Betraying Mike proved to be more than she bargained for, but she also could not bear to think about how the world would view her with another woman. This was just not who she was. It went against her upbringing, her religion, her values. She could so easily imagine the stern faces of the parents of Andy and Amy's playmates, imagine them monitoring their children's exposure to the Fournier household. She could feel her mother and father's unshakable anger and damnation. They would no doubt refuse to meet Lily. And she owned her own business, for God's sake. When word got out, her employees would diminish their respect for her and they would gossip in secret whispers, *"Did you know she's a lesbian?"* they would say. *"That explains why she never wears skirts."* They would tell her new employees first thing, and maybe even their business associates and Alex's power in the world would diminish, and shortly after that she would lose her swagger.

Her sister Paula disapproved from the start. A year later her complaints had heightened. "You're spending too much time with that friend of yours. What's up with the two of you?" she had admonished. At the time, although it was totally out of character, Alex did not respond at all. She did not tell Paula how integral she and Lily had become to one another. But several hours later, she told Lily the trip to Paris was a go. It was the least she could do to make amends for her complicit and silent betrayal.

25

They checked in at Logan Airport giggling like third grad-
ers on their first bus trip. Just before boarding Air France
Flight 337, Alex called home and promised Andy and
Amy a vast supply of postcards and gifts throughout her
trip. Leaving Mike and the kids had not been easy. Alex
worried about and struggled with guilt and uncertainty.
But she also felt exhilarated: like Lily, after months of
unspoken and forward moving intimacy, she grasped the
reality of what neither of them would clearly and defini-
tively understand for another year.

From start to finish Flight 337 had predictably inad-
equate leg room and bare bone service. The seven hour
flight should have been uncomfortable but it was any-

thing but. Lily and Alex talked non-stop about everything from politics to poltergeist, nibbled on sliced cheese and apples and crackers and truffles cleverly anticipated by Lily and in between took turns resting their heads on each other's shoulders. Stepping off the plane and into the ancient bustle of the Roissy Charles DeGaulle Airport, Alex could hardly contain herself. She was as giddy and wonderstruck as a five year old as they pushed and prodded themselves through a riotous and wild confluence of hundreds of travelers converging from all directions into one single file customs line.

Lily pulled out the instruction sheet from Show of the Month and headed toward a sign that said *Transport au sol.* There she found a large white phone and in her adequate French told the operator that the Peterson-Fournier party had arrived. They were directed curbside and along with eight other travelers they squeezed into a Renault mini van, where a gregarious Parisian driver talked, pointed and laughed throughout the forty-five minute ride from the airport to the heart of Paris, upon which he delivered each group to the doorstep of their hotel.

Show of the Month offered dozens of three star accommodations, and Lily had looked at every one before she chose the Hotel Moderne Saint-Germain. Located in the 6th Arrondissement on the Left Bank, within a block of the Sorbonne and easy walking distance to the Latin Quarter, it was an old world charmer with forty-five rooms on four floors. The lobby was sliced into three small sections. To the left, the front desk and concierge, in the middle a glitzy bright sitting area where a group of Japanese tourists had spread out and were talking non-stop, and to the right a cozy breakfast room where Lily and Alex would start each of their seven days with a croissant, raspberry jam, ham and cheese, orange juice, and a double cappuccino.

Just beyond the reception desk, Lily and Alex and their two large suitcases tightly squeezed into an old gold elevator. Once inside they turned the round brass dial to number two and manually pulled shut the crisscross doors. Then with the push of a button the heavy elevator doors thudded closed and an abrupt jolt catapulted them upward until it stopped just as abruptly. The doors opened and they stepped into to a dimly lit hallway. They walked fifteen steps to Room 214, turned the oversized key, and there they were.

Lily and Alex entered the room with the same elementary school giggles that began in Boston. Alex flicked on a light to reveal a tiny room with grey walls, two twin beds pushed together, each covered with a thin clean worn wool pink blanket, a small night table, and one maple four drawer dresser. A sink was tucked into the far right corner of the room opposite a splinter of a closet at the opposite end. In between the two, a doorway opened to a clean efficient bathroom that somehow managed to fit in a toilet, shower and bidet.

Lily and Alex looked at one another and burst into laughter.

"Cozy, eh, Madame?" Alex said.

"Very very cozy, c'est très parfait," Lily responded.

Lily walked across the room and looked out onto a small balcony one floor above the bustling Avenue St. Germain.

"Alex!" she beckoned. "The view is fantastic."

Newcomers to Paris are surprised by the pervading grayness of the city and its concrete architecture. It's not until they figure out how to focus on the street level that the vibrant colors and rich history truly unfolds. Lily knew this already, Alex did not, but it did not take long for them to scan in delightful unison the ornate concrete upper stories of every building and then let their eyes savor the sidewalk scene below. They would be entertained by its contrasts of pulsating color and movement, the storefronts, awnings, flower boxes, fresh fruits and vegetables, café tables, umbrellas, men and women carrying French bread and riding bicycles.

"It's so Paris, Lily," Alex gushed.

"Oui," Lily said, "c'est très parfait."

Alex laughed, "Lily, I hope you know how to say more than that."

"Oui," Lily said, "je peux dire que nous allons avoir une semaine fabuleuse."

"Oh you show-off. What does that mean, besides the fabulous part?"

"It means we are going to have a fabulous fantastic wonderful terrific week."

"Oui, oui," said Alex, "oui, oui, oui."

Lily lifted Alex's suitcase onto one of the twin beds and placed her own on the other. She leaned over and began organizing her clothes and toiletries. Alex approached her from behind. She put her arms around Lily's waist and tucked her head so it nestled into Lily's shoulder.

"Honey girl," Alex said, "will you sleep with me tonight?"

Lily stiffened. She turned around and looked directly at Alex.

"You think?" she asked.

"Yes," Alex said, "I do think."

"Whoa. Wow," Lily said. She waited a few seconds and continued, "Okay." She paused again.

"Okay," she said, "so our tour on the Seine starts at one, then we'll find that stationary store we read about, then stroll until we find a fabulous café for dinner, and finish day one with banana and chocolate crepes. Then pick up some wine and come back to the world's smallest room and see if these twin beds really will stay together." Another pause. "Okay?"

"Yes," said Alex, smiling. "That is what we'll do, Lily. That's exactly what we'll do."

26

There was more to Alex's letter, but Lily had stopped reading. Her mind flittered and paced, bewildered, astonished, terrified.

What do you mean Alex, 'I'm still here'? Do you mean you will stay with your family and try to welcome me back into your life? Or that you want to be with me, live with me, bring along your Fiesta ware and winter boots? Do you mean it will be okay when I touch you, or that you will still shudder from the stern catholic guilt of loving me in this way?

Logical, practical, steady Lily at that moment apparently had an out of body experience, overtaken by a sudden improbable impossible flash in front of her. It looked exactly like those yellow lightening zigzags you see in the comic strips: a massive bolt thundering down from her ceiling, there in solid form, right before her eyes. She shook her head.

Could it ever be that she and Alex would really be together, deal with her illness together, sleep and eat together, watch *Wheel of Fortune* every night together? And if so, could they ever make things right with Alex's husband and children, with Max, with their parents and siblings? Would Andy and Amy remember her? Would they hate her? Would they still laugh when she sang her John Denver songs? Would they still ask her to make bacon and eggs topped with her Uncle John's salsa recipe?

Could she and Alex hold on to each other tight and true this time, and in the darkness, just as Letterman began his monologue, find the safe haven they could not find before, even when it was right in front of them?

Then another zigzag flash: *Alex would die.* She would return and Lily's life would be upside down and inside out and ecstatic and whole, and then, just as quickly, Alex would die. Or even worse she would return ambivalent and guilt-ridden and then she would die. She would earnestly try as she had done for the three years before the end, and she would fail, whimpering by night and wringing by day, respectively begging Mike and Jesus Christ to forgive her and take her back.

Lily put Alex's letter back in the top right hand drawer of her dresser. She tucked it under her favorite knee-highs, and she patted it slowly and gently before she shut the drawer and walked away. She would be sufficiently composed before she read about the ending her soul mate was proposing.

27

Anyone who knows will tell you that chemotherapy is poison. You feel it running through your veins like a blow torch gone wild.

Alex would complete six cycles of chemotherapy in all, each lasting twenty-one days. Before the start of each, she was required to prepare the week before, which happened to be the last week of a current cycle, thus beginning the wretched process all over again: medication for anxiety and another for nausea, steroids, and fast moving Benadryl. Then her body would suffer the miserable indignity of eight hours being filled with IV bags labeled *'Do not come in contact with human skin'*. Even in her pathetic state, Alex noticed that the oncology nurses would never start or finish the process without wearing protective gloves at all times.

After she heard the diagnosis Alex spent three days hidden under swollen eyes and mindful terror, but then, true to form, she got cracking. She arranged for her marketing director, a trustworthy young man with a future to build, to handle the management of her company for the next few months. She studied the kitchen calendar to be sure that each of Andy and Amy's academic, performance, social and extracurricular activities and needs were planned for and in place. She made a quick trip to her parents' in Rhode Island. She made sure the kids understood that they needed to be uncharacteristic angels, in her words, until they could all get through this, and she did her best to comfort Mike, who at this early stage seemed almost catatonic.

"Mike," she said one night as they got into bed, "what can I do?"

"Don't die," he pleaded. She knew he was clenching his pillow.

"Mike," Alex said, "don't think about that. Think that I am going to be nagging you to paint the garage and take down the Christmas lights. Or think that I will withhold sex the next time you drink too much."

He reached for her. Alex put her arms around her husband and for the only time she could remember his muscular frame felt thin and slight.

"Some people do survive," she said.

Now in the darkness of their bed, she knew he was crying.

"Mike." That's all she could say. She centered her breathing and brought him into her. In the months ahead he would recall the way she said his name that night, and she was glad that he would remember that his wife loved him.

28

"You haven't finished the letter? How could you possibly not finish it?" Wendy asked. "Besides, what difference does it make? It's not like you're going to drop everything and give up your life again."

When she looked at Lily's blank face and saw that the expected response was not coming, she said, "Lily, you can't be serious."

Silence.

"Lily, talk to me."

"I still love her, Wendy."

"But what about Max?" Wendy's voice was rising to plea level.

"I told Max I needed time," Lily's voice cracked.

Wendy put her arm around her friend's shoulder in an effort to steady them both. She tried to sound calm.

"But no matter how this might turn out, it can't be good for you, right?"

More silence.

"Isn't that right?" Wendy repeated.

Lily's face was a combination of schoolyard guilt and adult remorse. She swallowed before speaking, "The last seven years, Wendy, it's been hell. I comforted myself by believing it was no different than adjusting to someone you love dying and having to go on because there is no other choice. And yes, I've settled in. Yes, I have a good life. I love Max, no doubt about it, but not in the way that I'll always love Alex. I fell in love with Alex almost the moment I met her. I can still feel the breeze from the river the first night we went out, the way it felt when we walked into the restaurant together."

Wendy tried another tact. "Lily, do you think it's helpful for you to reminisce about her? She left you and you haven't heard from her in years. And she's very sick. Where can that go, Lily?"

Lily shook her head. "I don't know. I don't know what she wants. Maybe this is just a farewell letter and that'll be that." She began to cry, small tears streaming in a straight line down both cheeks. Wendy opened her purse and handed her a Kleenex.

"I worry about you with this." Wendy's voice was now an equal mix of tact and sympathy.

"I know, I understand, but I still love her. I can't kid myself about that. I've never stopped loving her. When I saw that envelope, even before I opened the letter, it all came back as though no time had passed at all. And I don't think I could walk away if she needs me."

"Oh dear God, Lily. It's déjà vu."

"Yes," Lily said, "and I might be okay with that."

"And if it's the same shit all over again?" Wendy watched Lily regain her composure.

"Well, I hope I'd recover and move on. But maybe it won't be the same shit, Wendy. Maybe it will be destiny straightening itself out."

"Oh dear God," Wendy said again. "This is not you, Lily. You're more level headed than this. You could be crazy you know. This is magical thinking. Still, I hate to admit it but I kind of understand where you're coming from. Maybe we're both crazy."

"Maybe," Lily said, "and maybe not."

29

Several weeks had passed since Lily first held Alex's letter. She had read most of it, but not the final paragraph. She simply could not bear to face information that might disrupt, dishevel, dishearten, perhaps even destroy everything it had taken her years to recraft. If you had asked her twenty-two days ago, Lily would have confidently told you that this was no longer possible. After all, she would go days, weeks even without thinking of Alex at all. She had stopped including her in her prayers, and she no longer revisited all the *'what ifs'* that life had thrown at her broken parts–so many coming at her with such speed that she'd repeatedly forgotten to duck.

But today, at a moment when memory was intersecting with instinct, Lily was again unsure she would remember to duck. It wasn't that she hadn't learned to swerve. There was no way to avoid occasionally hearing about Alex, but her friends knew to avoid the subject altogether and on the occasion when a casual acquaintance mentioned that Alex's business had grown to a dozen employees, or that Andy had made the baseball regionals, or that Mike's company was being bought out by Warren Buffet, Lily would simply shrug her shoulders and say, "Yes, isn't that wonderful?"

Only once had she carelessly risked an actual encounter with Alex: she was at the New England Executive Woman's Conference and mid-way through she realized how easily Alex could be there too. Quickly she had scanned the room, checked the attendance list, and made note of all the exit doors. Only then, carefully, had she tucked away her vigilance.

But that kind of slip was rare. Lily fastidiously and consciously took active steps to move on and forget. She did this because she believed this was best for both of them, and she was positive this was best for herself. The result of her efforts–a professional woman's version of underground hiding–had paid off.

That is, until three weeks ago.

In three week's time, Lily's life had been overturned in ways she could not believe. She found herself unable to focus and concentrate in class. Her eight hours of solid sleep had whittled down to five or six. She began mind-lessly pacing from the kitchen to living room, weighing every possible consequence of her response, or non-response to Alex's letter. She had not been able to bring herself to finish it. She couldn't bear the possibility that the letter was another apology, a mea culpa, nothing more. Such a heavy price for another unexpected total overhaul of her life.

Still, Lily knew she had to read the letter. And she also knew she might again sacrifice for Alex. What she did not know was what Alex might hope for and ask for; and therefore how much of her own sanity the sacrifice might extract.

Some things were clear: if Alex still loved her, told her so, and wanted to see her, she could not say no. And if it was clear that the purpose of the letter was no more than a reaching out to an old friend, she would probably say no and then deal with the effects of the raw loss all over again. But she did not know what she would do if Alex's penance was yet again ambivalent, a dying woman she loved so fully who still loved her wanting, needing to wrap up loose ends, but only able to do so at the periph-ery of her day-to-day life. That would bring all the pain rushing back. Lily didn't know if she could survive that again.

Now, on a Sunday morning at 7:43 am, Lily sat on her bed with Alex's scribbly handwriting in front of her. She had just one remaining paragraph to read.

She stared at the last page of the letter for several minutes before she reached for her reading glasses and placed them on the rim of her nose. She glanced to be sure her warm cup of tea was on the nightstand where she had left it.

Then, at 7:46 Lily finished the letter.

"All this time I've wondered if I could or would truly accept never seeing you again. I've always known how badly I hurt you, but it's been a slow painful miserable process for me to truly grasp the cost to myself. Ambivalence is a terrible way to live, Lily. I wouldn't wish it on anyone. But somewhere in between hearing my diagnosis and re-evaluating my life, my struggle stopped. Just like that. It's a hell of a time to tell you, Lily—I can only imagine what you are thinking as you read this. Here I am a sick, possibly terminal, pretty hairless, thin-to-the bones pathetic facsimile of myself contacting you at the worse possible time, I know. It's complicated, it takes giant balls on my part to do this now, but here's what it is Lily: I've never really left, and if you're willing, I would like to be where you are.

Love Always,
Alex"

Heat rushed to Lily's cheeks. She was cast back to her first ride on the merry-go-round in Martha's Vineyard: five year old terrified Lily, sitting four feet atop of that moving carved horse with the giant teeth, spinning up and down, around and around until the merry-go-round stopped and she tried to stand only to find out that her legs were rubber, unable to hold her up. She was now forty-three year old Lily, on that horse again, trying to stand on rubber legs that would not hold her up. She put the letter back in her underwear drawer and sat on her bed for what seemed like hours. Then, finally, slowly, weakly, she stood up, put on her sweats, grabbed Louie and Sadie's leash, and without catching her breath, pushed the three of them toward the river for a long walk.

It was unreal. *Alex,* she kept repeating, *Oh, God, Alex.* She shook her head, barely able to consider even the molecule of possibility that Alex might really be back. Then, with the sun in front of her, with Louie delighted by the quickened pace and Sadie predictably panting by the second go-round, with the path eerily calm, Lily, competent, clear headed, studious, serious, reliable Lily, let the tears and anguish and loneliness and regret that she had carried all these years spill forth with the power of a hurricane. She no longer held back the strength of her sadness. Ten years from the first day she saw Alex standing before her in that cream colored hallway, Lily would once again never be the same.

30

Sometimes cancer blasts in like a paratrooper, and sometimes it tiptoes in, a secret intruder poised to steal your life. In Alex's case, it did both. Normally healthy and possessing high energy, Alex had the flu, then could not shake the aftermath. It was only normal that her breathing and stamina would be affected for a while. But after she backed out of three tennis dates, and after a month of failed antibiotics and escalating hoarseness, her family physician ordered a chest x-ray, and then a CAT scan.

It took less than a week before Alex was referred to an oncologist. "There's some concern, it's not clear. Let's play it safe," her family physician had said. "Dr. Chambliss is the expert. Let's see what he has to say."

Alex and Mike spent a short-fused weekend keeping busy driving Amy to her dance lessons, dropping Andy and his friends off at the movies, grocery shopping, fixing dinner, fixing the back doorbell, making love, making small talk, until Monday morning at 8 am, when they sat across from Dr. Mark Chambliss, Chief Oncologist at the New England Cancer Institute.

"I'm sorry to confirm it is lung cancer, Alex," Dr. Chambliss said.

Neither fear nor faith can quite protect you from certain news. Alex and Mike both gasped. Mike looked straight ahead and tightened his shoulders. Alex put her hand across her mouth, as if to hold back a horrid bile.

She wondered how many times had he said these words to how many other people. And whatever he would say next, how many of those other people lived, survived, thrived after this moment and this day that they could never, would never, forget?

"We'll treat it with a combination of radiation and chemotherapy. I'd like to begin next week."

Alex stared at Mike and then down at her clenched hands, which had ripped the Kleenex she was holding to shreds.

"Whoa. Jesus. What stage is it, Dr. Chambliss?" she asked.

"It's stage three."

Alex knew what this meant. Still, she stared at him and said, "What are my chances? I want to know."

"Well," the doctor said, "twenty-five percent of patients with stage three lung cancer survive two years or more. There's no reason you can't be included in that twenty-five percent." Alex saw him hesitate, looking at her and Mike to gauge how much information they really wanted.

"Look," he said, "I just saw a patient who was diagnosed four years ago. She's in remission and feeling fine. It's not always that way, but you're young, strong, feisty. It's non small cell lung cancer in a single site. We can treat this, Alex. We will treat this. You're not a candidate for surgical resection so we'll go in with radiation therapy in combination with chemotherapy. You'll feel terribly sick, you won't be the belle of any balls, but we'll aim to knock it out."

In an instant, stunned and stupefied, without sound or movement, Alex heard a wailing moan deep deep inside her head. *"Oh Amy, oh Andy, oh Mike, oh Mom and Dad, oh Lily,"* it cried. *"Oh Lily, oh Lily, oh Lily."*

31

Three days after finishing the first letter, rushing to get to her first period class and simultaneously driving and sifting through the mail she had snatched on her way out the door, Lily was shocked to find another cursively distinctive letter. Despite her tardiness, she pulled into the far corner of Trader Joe's parking lot, slowly opened the envelope, and unfolded a single sheet of linen paper with its signature swirl and curl lettering.

"Hey!" the letter began, *"Okay, so you haven't responded. I know you, Lily—you would communicate somehow if you definitely did not/could not/would not want to see me. So I'm now forced to revert to Plan B.*

I'm enclosing a ticket for the Queen City hullabaloo. It's still at Mount Holyoke. Remember when we went, Lily? I'll be wearing the same outfit. I'll be looking for you. This ticket is not cheap. Come on now...

Love Alex"

32

At four o'clock on an ordinary Saturday afternoon, barely
a year after first meeting, pelting rain interfering with their
shopping plans, Alex sat on Lily's couch, her legs propped
on the coffee table in front of her. Lily was nearby, bal-
ancing on the arm of the couch. When she reached for her
glass of chardonnay on the table in front of her, she fell
over like a beanie baby and found herself on top of Alex.
Their startle response was quickly replaced by raucous
laughter, and in the midst of their awkward entangling,
Alex leaned down and kissed Lily. When Lily hesitated
and pulled back, Alex kissed her again. This time Lily
cupped Alex's face with both hands, and they kissed for a
very long time, short and then deep kisses.

Lily spoke first. "Alex, I don't mean to be seducing you. I mean, is this okay?"

Alex locked onto Lily's eyes. "It's too late now, Lily. It's beyond okay." She grinned and nudged them both down on the couch so their bodies stretched out beside one another, ruler tight with no space between them. They kissed again, their hips thrusting and pushing together, their cheeks feeling the tiny hairs on each other's skin, their hands exploring in a free form dance that left them both breathless.

Two hours later, soaked and spent, they lay motionless in each other's arms until Lily kissed the tip of Alex's nose.

"Oh my God," Alex said, "oh my God, Lily. That was incredible."

Lily looked at her. "Alex," she said, "I love you."

Alex grinned. "Is the pope catholic, Lily? Don't you know I love you too?"

33

Alex did not intend to fall in love with Lily. In the beginning, she accepted she had stumbled upon the unique good fortune of a soul mate best friend. When passion was added to the mix, she viewed their sex as a curious experiment. And when it continued, because there was no wish or ability to stop it, she tried to justify their intimacy as a natural extension of loving deeply.

And besides, she cherished a lot more about their relationship than the sex. Lily had taken root in the most mundane parts of her life. She was quietly present to help her balance her checkbook, write the marketing brochure, lift Andy past Pesky Pole at Fenway Park, help Mike plan the camping trip to Acadia, chuckle at Alex's advance complaints about bugs and bathroom-less toilets.

There was a romantic playfulness between them that Alex loved. One weekend when she stayed at Lily's when Mike and the kids were visiting his parents in San Diego, Alex would leave little cards and notes under the toaster, on top of the pillow, some of them so corny or riotous that she could hear Lily laughing three rooms away. *'I love you more than shoes'*, one said; another, *'We've been through a lot together, and most of it was your fault'*.

If Lily and Alex had become lovers, so be it, Alex thought, but every minute of every day she reminded herself that they were also so much more.

Alex told her tennis partner and good friend Liz about Lily two months after their stormy Saturday afternoon on the Crate and Barrel couch. The two friends had finished a challenging tennis match with this aggressive woman Alex called Allison Bitch and her spidery partner Nancy. Pumped up and hungry, they headed for the Esselon café.

It was perhaps the atmosphere and association that caused Alex to spill the news. "Liz," she began, "I want to tell you something but I need you to swear you'll keep it confidential. Like never tell not another soul, ever."

Liz nodded. "You know I'm good at that. No problem."

Alex tried to speak but nothing came out. It was an odd sensation for her, almost a temporary paralysis. She tried again but all she could do was clear her throat and say "Oh gosh."

Liz was no dummy. Besides she was an MSW counselor whose first marriage ended in divorce due to her own infidelity. She knew the signs.

"Alex," she drawled, "are you going to tell me you're having an affair?"

Relief all over her face, the words came gushing out. "I wouldn't call it an affair, Liz. It's actually worse than that. I've fallen in love." There was a confused tenderness in her voice.

"Okay," Liz said, "who is he?"

Alex was not prepared for this part. How could she explain this? How would Liz react? Was she making a mistake putting words to this at all?

"Well, someone who's bright and kind and attractive and interesting and healthy and who I can't stop thinking about, every minute, almost."

"Do I know him, Alex?" Liz asked.

Alex sighed. There was no way around using the right pronoun.

"It's not a him, Liz. It's a her."

Liz flinched. "A woman? Wow. Am I surprised?" she asked herself out loud. "I think so," she said. "Did you know?"

"Did I know I could fall in love with a woman? No, no I didn't. Maybe if I was totally honest with myself I'd admit I've had crushes on a few women going all the way back to my 3rd grade teacher. But no, I wasn't looking for a woman or anyone for that matter. But I was drawn to her from the moment I met her. She's a wonderful person."

"Does she love you too?" Liz asked.

"Yes," Alex said softly. "We love each other."

"What about Mike? Does he know?"

"Liz! No, he doesn't know. What am I supposed to say, 'By the way honey, Lily and I are in love and the sex is awesome.'" Alex stopped. Stunned, she brought her hands together in front of her. In an instant, she had replaced the joy of acknowledging Lily with the guilt of cheating on Mike.

"Oh Jesus, Liz. When I'm with her it is so easy to forget that what I'm doing is wrong. So easy. And when I'm with Mike all I can think about is her."

Liz put down her fork and looked sympathetically at her friend. "Do you think you might be a lesbian? That would explain a lot of this."

Alex shook her head and dropped her shoulders. "I don't know. I don't even know how I feel about that. The kids would freak. My parents. My business. My upbringing even. I have enough problems accepting how I feel about Lily without tackling all the rest of it."

"But you're sure you love her?" Liz asked.

"Oh yes," Alex answered. "I love her."

Liz was quiet for a moment and then said, "When I cheated on Steve, it turned out that it was more about not being happy with him than it was about wanting to be with someone else. Maybe you need time to sort that part out."

"Time or no time, I'm playing with fire, right?"

"Kind of. Well, yes," Liz replied, "But sometimes that's just the way it is. Sometimes you can't change even what you wish you could change. And we both know love is powerful."

"But so is duty and honor. This isn't fair to Mike and the kids, I know that."

"Well," Liz said, "maybe that's the part you'll truly need to deal with. Maybe you'll need to tell Mike what's going on, so he isn't made a fool of, you know, even if you're not sure what you want."

"Even if telling him will definitely threaten my marriage and family?"

"Alex, that part's already happened. It seems to me it's the guilt and honor you need to handle. And you need to be kind to yourself. These things happen. Sometimes for the better. Don't beat yourself up."

"Is it possible I could love her for life like this?"

"Definitely," Liz said. "Maybe she's your spiritual partner. Then again, maybe it's just sex. Give yourself time. Alex. And don't forget you are a good person." Liz thought a moment. "Are you sure you want to keep seeing her?"

The question elicited visible pain on Alex's face. "Liz, I can't imagine not seeing her. I'd be miserable. And so would she."

"Then I think the issue really is about what you share and don't share with your husband."

Alex opened her purse and put her credit card on top of the check. "Thanks, Liz," she said. "I needed to tell someone."

"Anytime Alex." Liz put her hand on her friend's shoulder. "I feel for you," she said. "I really do."

34

One weekend in August, Lily and Alex are beaching it at Herring Cove, lying on a blue and red towel with a giant illustration of Betty Boop in the middle. They are side by side at the public but clearly designated "gay" stretch of the Cape Cod National Seashore, lulled by the sound of three foot waves roaring in and then out again, and warmed by the 85 degree sun on their skin. They hear distant voices and conversations all around them, not quite able to pick up the details but the festivity of the moment is clear and decisive.

Situated at the tip of Cape Cod and the Massachusetts boot and surrounded by the Atlantic Ocean, Provincetown is a quaint little fishing village turned art colony turned

Coney Island funk. A high percentage of the real estate tax bills still go to the many Catholic Portuguese families with deep roots in the fishing industry, but times have changed the town and its texture. Affluent gay and lesbian professionals have scooped up properties and converted them to condos, transforming the community into a backlog of part time residences. This has magnified a tension that has always existed between the straight and gay community, but it hasn't changed the fact that Provincetown has always been and still remains a Mecca for artists, bohemians, homosexuals and anyone else who finds him/herself there at the ocean's edge for reasons of anonymity, splendor, solitude, sexual, or creative desire.

No matter who you are or what your story is, you will be greeted with a laisse faire welcome mat in Provincetown. In high season the town population swells to 20,000 and in off season it shrinks back to its 3000-4000 year-rounders. The vast encompassing magnificent Atlantic Ocean, visible everywhere you look, dominates. And so does the outrageous and real freedom to simply be yourself. The far reaching and calming effect the town has on its inhabitants and visitors probably comes from the rhythm of the sea, or maybe from a tolerance stretched to the limit, but whatever the reasons, this is a place to find or lose yourself, and even the most hardened souls get that.

Along the three mile stretch of Commercial Street, which runs parallel to the bay side of the ocean, same sex couples slowly walk hand-in-hand and throw their heads back in safe laughter. Writers hole up in 300 square foot studio space with white stained driftwood floors and the wild ocean tides just steps away. And at the upper level of the Mews Restaurant, a fifty-six year old middle school principal dressed in a Liz Claiborne skirt and a frilly white blouse sips his martini and proudly shows off his ruby red nail polish.

For most of the day Lily and Alex alternate between bobbing in the weightless salt water waves and lying next to each other on their Betty Boop towel, the cool skin of their arms and legs reassuringly touching. Later they will have a disastrously unsatisfying lobster dinner at Clem and Ursies, walk hand-in-hand along the Court Street Bay, recalling every silly thing they have ever done together, and fall asleep in a king sized bed in a pitch black room with the soft safe glow of twinkle stars every which way around them.

35

Lily's heart cartwheeled as she walked the thirty or so steps leading to the entrance of the Mount Holyoke Women's Center. She handed her ticket to an overly gleeful woman dressed in blue taffeta and a purple and orange speckled scarf around her neck. She checked her coat and dropped a dollar in the tip jar. She then looked straight ahead, straightened her purse, swallowed hard, and walked through the doors into a huge room with a twenty-five foot ceiling and giant black and white photographs of famous women covering the far left wall. The room was humming with hundreds of women, many huddled around three long tables in the center of the room, where dozens of appetizers had been tastefully prepared and arranged. Some women wore gowns, some tuxes, some dresses, others Ann Taylor pants with fitted blouses, a few jeans with slightly dressy sweaters. Lily had struggled before she chose a pale blue Liz Claiborne silk dress which fell just below her knees. She accessorized it with a thin black suede belt with short tassels hanging from it, and a blue and purple scarf tied loosely around her neck. She had purposely chosen black tights and black flats in case she had to quickly move in one direction or another.

The Queen City prom, as Lily and Alex had long ago dubbed it for no particular reason, was actually an annual fundraiser sponsored by Mount Holyoke College to benefit local women's shelters and services. Attended by several hundred women, most of them professionals in their field, the event was close to a black tie event in substance and style. This included a first class band–this year the Dykaroos–and a dance floor where couples and singles gaily swung to and fro, together and alone, unencumbered by the expectations of heterosexual decorum.

Lily had not attended Queen City since her break up with Alex. This had not been a good thing, given she was on the board of the women's center and rarely refused her money or presence in support of women and families. But this event was one of a few activities she simply could not do. She was confused and unsure why or how she had managed to come tonight. Entering the carnivorous room, her eyes scanned and darted every which way, looking for Alex, her five foot four inch 130 pound beloved former soul mate who had walked out on her by phone seven years ago and for some reason decided they should reconnect before she unceremoniously died.

Lily was concerned that her dress hung limply, which was pretty much how she felt internally. She had no idea what to do, how to walk, where to keep her hands, or what in the name of sweet Jesus she would even say to Alex, on the assumption, of course, that Alex was even there. *Maybe she isn't,* she thought, *she may have backed out, or been too sick.* The thought that she'd come and Alex had not was excruciating. Lily felt the familiar choke of abandonment all around her, and then she saw Paula.

Paula stood approximately sixty yards in front of her, nervously standing by herself in the far left corner of the room, looking like a nun at a Hugh Hefner convention. Lily wondered why Alex's heterosexual catholic sister would be here at all, but before her brain could compute a reason so obvious and simple, she spotted Alex. At first she appeared as a tiny speck, surrounded by dozens of animated heads towering above her, but there she was, seated, her head level with Paula's waist, staring straight ahead at the main door. *That's odd,* Lily thought, just before she realized Alex had to have seen her enter.

Lily was frozen. Still, she knew she had to move, so she took a rapid succession of small unsteady steps until Alex was directly in front of her. She stopped, immobilized, stunned. There she was: glorious hell bent Alex, in a wheelchair, a silk purple bandana around her head and large dangling silver hoop earrings, thin as a rail, pale and pasty, still radiant. Paula protectively stood beside her sister, looking like she might cry.

Once Lily had asked her orthopedic surgeon why she did not remember losing consciousness during arthroscopic surgery. He explained that although she had indeed been conscious and interactive for a full five minutes that she could not recall, her brain shut down before it could store this into memory. This was what was happening as she grasped the reality of seeing Alex. Her brain had totally shut down. She did not know until afterwards that she flung her purse on the floor and ran full speed ahead, welling tears obscuring her view, instinct leading her to Alex and her wheelchair. She was kneeling, her arms around Alex and her face buried into her collarbone. Lily understood precisely what was happening: for years she had been flying rudderless, waiting for a safe place to land. This and this alone was the place.

Alex fell forward, startled. Then she lifted her rail thin arms and locked them around Lily's neck. Without motion or sound, they were frozen in their embrace, comforted by the warmth of each other's skin, reclaiming scents and sensations so familiar it was as if no time had passed at all; as if they might stay this way forever, oblivious to everything around them.

Then, more like a chime than a cymbal, Alex laughed.

"Oh Lily, oh Lily," she whispered, "I imagined everything, over and over, but I never guessed that you would run like that. God, oh Lily." Alex pulled away, her eyes riveted on Lily. "Let me look at you," she said. "Oh my God, you've lost weight. You look terrific. Oh Lily." And then, as an afterthought, "I don't look so good, huh?"

Lily was speechless. She cleared her throat and tried to pull herself together. She did her best to muffle a quiet sob that only grew louder, and she wiped her eyes with her scarf. She tried to stand but Alex would have none of it.

"No Lily. No. Stay here. Hey," Alex said, "I bought you an apple martini. Here. Drink it fast. Then I'll buy you another."

"Alex," Lily cleared her throat again and began to speak.

"No Lily," Alex interrupted. "First let's remember who we are together. Then you can call me a stupid ass. And then we'll talk. Okay? Oh, and I'd like to let Paula leave this den of lesbians now as long as you don't mind helping me with my personal needs."

Lily threw her head back and laughed. "Jesus Alex," she said, "I don't even get a moment to fall apart before I have to be on bathroom duty?"

Alex grinned. "Life's a bitch. But then again sometimes you get the chance to do it right." She paused. "Oh, and Lily, my suitcase. Do you mind if we put it in your car?"

36

Alex shut off the hot water faucet and let an ice cold stream splash onto her face. Years ago, there had been weekends when she followed this routine hoping to wash away her guilt, but not so this morning. She was remotely sick and unsettled, but two nights ago she unpacked the contents of her suitcase into a five drawer oak dresser and laid out her toiletries and makeup in Lily's bathroom. Through the grey steam of her shower, she looked around in disbelief. For the first time, she was here without secrets. For the weeks and months that would follow, she would experience enveloping sadness thinking about her children, about Mike, about her illness, about the burden she was putting on them and on Lily, but she would no longer shrink from shame.

She wrapped an oversized towel around her, rubbed dry her fuzzed head, and slipped on the Minnie Mouse slippers that Amy had excitedly given her last Christmas. She walked down the hall to the living room and motioned to Lily, who was sitting on the couch, her feet propped on the cracked leather hassock.

"Hey honey girl," Alex said.

Lily looked up from her book and smiled. "How was your shower?"

"Good. Great." Alex paused. "Lily, do you know how much I love you?"

Lily nodded. "I do. I love you so much too."

"Are you sure you're up for this?"

This is the question that can never go away, a clear question with no chance of a clear answer. Still, Lily nodded.

"Yes," she said, "but I worry about you. I don't know if you should be away from the kids, even away from Mike. I'm here, Alex. I'm with you no matter what. But we can't have you struggling about where you should be, worrying about Andy and Amy…and…"

Alex stretched out and lay her head on Lily's lap. "Lily," she began, "Andy was ten, Amy was nine when you and I stopped seeing each other. I went to counseling, I went to confession, I buried myself in my work, I tried to be parent of the year."

She pushed her words forward. "And I tried to be a devoted wife. I never questioned my obligation and responsibility to my family. I knew I could never live with myself if I abandoned Mike and the kids, no matter how much I loved you. There was really no choice: the kids needed me, the guilt would have destroyed me."

Lily caressed Alex's face with the back of her fingers, across her forehead and down to her chin and back. She responded slowly, thoughtfully. "Alex, how are we going to make this work? I can't imagine that seeing the kids twice a week will be enough, and what happens when they need you, when there's a problem at home?"

Alex shook her head. "Remember when Mike cheated on me in San Francisco, Lily, long before you and I met? It was a one night stand, he said it meant nothing. But my cheating, I could never say it meant nothing. I could no more reason or control my love for you than I could stop breathing. Maybe I couldn't get past the shame and guilt but the love, it meant everything."

Alex was a breath or two away from being unable to speak. Her words tripped as she struggled for composure. "I can tell you exactly how I'm going to be away from Andy and Amy. One word: torture. But Lily, when I heard that diagnosis, some colossal shift occurred, up one side and down the other. I could no longer accept living, or dying for that matter, without you. Like my dues were finally paid. Like it was now or never."

Alex forced a chuckle. "Which it probably is."

"Alex…" Lily said.

Alex stopped her. "No, please Lily, I need to say this. All my life I've struggled to do the right thing, and when I had kids I finally just knew what the right thing was. I can't think of anything I wouldn't do for them. I can't imagine dying before they're grown. I think about their dates and friends and graduations from high school and college, their weddings, their own children... to think that I might not be there, how will they possibly survive without me? I've written cards to them for their graduations and weddings and babies and given them to my sister just in case. And I've talked to them a lot about all of this. I let them know I might not be here but I am doing every fricking thing I can to come out of this whole. I've told them where to look for me in the night sky if that's what it comes down to." Alex dropped her voice as if to let Lily in on a secret. "I'll be one of those stars."

She pushed her head further into Lily's lap and continued. "I don't think it's possible for either of them to grasp how I could love and need you this much, how I could ever leave their father and our home. I can't explain it either. And I don't want to. I just know that I belong with you–that whatever time I have, it has to include you. It's just that simple now."

She kissed Lily's hand. "And you know what, Lily? Here's the bottom line. I would want my kids to do the same thing for themselves in their lives, if that's what it came to."

Lily's voice shook. "Alex, we won't lose each other again. Not ever. I swear to you we won't. But do you…"

"Lily," Alex spoke firmly. "I was drowning. Remember what you said the first night we met, when I asked you about obligation and responsibility?"

Lily nodded. "If you can't swim…" She stared at her earnest partner and smiled.

Alex returned the nod. "I never forgot that advice," she said. "I believe there'll come a time when the kids come around and are comfortable here, accepting of us. Either way I am their mother and they know that. I know they do. It's been seven agonizing years, Lily. I haven't felt whole for one moment in all that time. And the thought of you without me is worse than the thought of me without you. I've come to you sick and weak. I can't tell you I'll be around when your book is published or that we'll retire together to some little island somewhere with our magazines and martinis. I know it's a terrible time to ask you to commit to me again, but I'm full of love, Lily, and I will take care of you however I can for as long as I live."

That Sunday morning on a cocoa colored brushed suede couch, their bodies motionless, while Paul Simon sang 'Graceland' in the background, Lily and Alex held on to one another for a very long time.

When Alex finally sat up she looked directly at Lily. "If I should die, I'll keep the light on for you. Don't forget that."

Lily shook her head. "Alex, that is so hokey trite," she said. "But still, it's good to know."

37

Lily did not easily spill her emotions. Anyone who met her would be struck first by her intelligence, then her poise, and then her kindness, but not unnoticed would also be a calm exterior that assured that this is a person you would want on a desert island with you, or stuck on a elevator, or sitting beside you in the intensive care waiting room. Lily was not emotional, per se, but her demeanor, and her compassion, were steady and real.

When Lily called Mike, she had rehearsed what she wanted to convey. But it was all so impossible that she found herself holding on to the coffee table while she dialed the Fournier family number.

"Mike, it's Lily."

Silence.

"I don't know if it's even right to make this call, and I know you must hate me a thousand times over, but...I was wondering...could we meet, Mike?"

"Why, Lily?" Mike's tone was not closed tight but clearly wrapped in self protection.

"Mike, I don't know how—even if—we can make this work and I will do anything I can to make it easier. You, the kids, Alex, I wish I could..."

"What, Lily? You wish it had never happened? Well, I wish that too. But you thought about that too late."

Lily's started to speak, stopped, and then quietly said, "Mike, will you meet me?"

"Where?"

"Houghs?"

"When?"

"You tell me Mike and I'll be there."

"Let's get it over with. Tonight at six?"

Lily paused. She had not expected this and she would have to make arrangements so Alex would not be alone.

"Yes, Mike, tonight at six. Thank you, Mike."

38

The first night was soft with hope and rich with memory. If they hadn't known better, Lily and Alex could not be convinced that years had passed since they had lay beside one another, now embraced by a compassionate fate.

"Are you sure this is alright?" Lily whispered.

"Yes, I'll need to catch my breath, that's all," Alex whispered back.

Initially Lily moved tentatively, careful of a fragility she did not know. But there was no need for relearning. They pushed forward together, holding each other tightly and breathing in unison. Alex let Lily guide them until they lay side by side, two little vessels with no past and no moor left to separate them, no questions left to answer, no boundaries left to navigate, no distant shore left to long for.

When they looked up, they were both crying.

"Man, this beats crying alone," Alex said.

"Alex," Lily responded, "This beats everything."

Alex looked at Lily. "Honey girl, do you mind if we leave the light on tonight?"

Lily was puzzled. "Sure," she said, "but why?"

Alex kissed the bottom of her ear. "If I should wake up tonight, I want to know I'm not dreaming."

Lily smiled. "Then that's all there is to it. The light stays on."

39

Mike was seated in a corner booth furthest from the bar. When Lily walked in, he raised his right hand and motioned to her and she walked toward him, trying to steady herself by consciously keeping her knees straight. She pushed her purse and coat to the end of the seat across from Mike. She sat down and picked up a fork before she looked at him. When they finally made eye contact, she noticed his eyes were tentative, weak. He clenched several paper napkins in his left hand, twisting them tightly in front of him, until he noticed, even in the dim light of Hough's Tavern, Lily's face. She was close to crying herself.

They looked at each other and said nothing. Mike was braced, Lily was tight. Finally, she said, "Mike, I didn't mean for this to happen. I've never in my life been involved with someone who was already committed, and I've asked myself a thousand times why..."

"Stop, Lily. I'm not interested in your doing penance at my expense. I'm here because Alex is sick and our children are involved. And our children need the adults to make this crazy situation tolerable. And Alex needs her strength to fight."

Mike stopped and cleared his throat. Lily could see he was afraid he would lose his grip. She watched him glance over to the bar where his friend Danny and a few of the other guys were pretending to ignore him.

"Mike, tell me what I can do. Please, tell me what you think is best."

Mike pulled out a piece of yellow lined paper from his pocket and unfolded it. He stared at it for about ten seconds, moving his eyes rapidly from top to bottom, side to side, like one of those old Smith Corona typewriters.

"Well, first off, Alex will be staying with you. She and I already talked about that. She wants to come home on weekends, you know when the kids are more likely to get in trouble, with cars and parties and all, but I don't see that, really. I don't think it's good for her to move around like that. So I thought it would be good if the kids had dinner with their mother at your house on Fridays, and maybe one other night...that is, if you can handle that."

"Of course, Mike," Lily hesitated, "will they come?"

Mike snapped impatiently. "Lily, they will come

because they love their mother. They need their mother. And she is sick. So yes, they will come. I'll make sure they'll come."

Lily said nothing.

Mike continued, "You have to understand the kids are pretty upset. If they're not nice to you, cut them some slack. And do whatever you can to spare Alex from feeling in the middle. I'm not able to do that, but surely you ought to be able to. As for myself, I don't want her agonizing about her decision. The more comfortable she is, the stronger she'll be to fight the cancer. And that's paramount. So I want you to know, not right now, but sometime, I will try to be in the same room with you. For the sake of my family. Just don't stick my face in it, Lily."

Lily's head snapped back. Mike lowered his voice. "Listen, I know you aren't out celebrating. But this has got to be easier for you than it is for me."

Lily looked at him. "Mike, I never intended for this to happen. I know you love each other. I will never interfere with that. I can't explain or excuse myself. For all these years I tried every minute to move on. I knew she was with such a good man, a good family. I wouldn't have interfered. I'm so sorry it's come to this. I love her too, Mike."

Mike straightened his back and shoulders. He stared at Lily. "Listen Lily, she's got to get herself to remission and stay there. Maybe someday we can all be the weirdo one-happy-family. Or maybe she'll..." He stopped, paused just a second. "The kids will come around. I know they will. And I know you will help her with her needs. But I just want to be sure we understand one another: I want Alex to live. I'll do what's needed to help her with that. As for the rest of this mess, I'll deal with it after."

He paused again. "Who will stay with her when you're at work?"

"I'm taking the rest of the semester off," Lily said. "The next semester too if I have to. I'm working on a book and I can write it from home. And Alex said the woman–Carmen, is it?–will continue to come."

"Good," Mike said. "She wakes up sometimes pretty disoriented. You'll need to keep an eye, okay?"

"Mike, you are an incredible man," Lily said.

Mike looked down at his paper.

"Chemo and the Healing Circles? Who's going to handle those? I could still do Thursday afternoons and Mondays."

Lily is crying.

"Mike, should she move back home with you? Tell me."

"No," he snapped. "Just don't leave her alone for now, okay?"

"I won't."

"Call me if you need to. See you around, okay?" With that, Mike forcefully nodded, tossed a twenty dollar bill on the table, picked up his jacket, nodded again, and headed to the bar, where Danny patted the empty stool next to him, pushing a straight up shot of Johnny Walker Blue Label scotch in front of him and motioning for him to sit down.

40

"Mom, I can't come tonight. Macy's having a sleepover. And Andy says he's not coming if I don't."

Alex hesitated and closed her eyes. This was to be the first time her children would visit her and Lily together and Amy was begging out.

"Well honey," Alex said, "okay, how about lunch here tomorrow?"

"No, Mom." Amy's tone was exasperating and punishing. "You know I have practice tomorrow."

"Honey, we need to see each other at least twice a week. That's what your dad and I worked out."

"Maybe you should have thought of that before you left us Mom." Alex could hear the pained crack in Amy's voice.

"Amy," Alex said. Her voice was tender. "If it's okay with Dad, Lily could drop me off Sunday morning and we could have breakfast as a family. Would that be okay?"

"But Dad said you aren't strong enough to come back and forth."

"This I can do, honey."

"Alright then," Amy said.

"But Amy, you'll come here for dinner next Wednesday, okay?"

"Yes, okay Mom. I'll tell Andy too." Amy was trying. She was furious and confused, too young to accept the juggling her mother's decision had forced upon her, but she was trying.

"And Amy…"

"Yeah?"

"Do not smoke or drink tonight. Don't even think about it. Your father and I will ground you for five years if you do."

"Okay Mom." Alex knew that Amy was smiling at this, affectionately tolerating her mother's nagging guidance.

"And Amy," Alex said.

"What, Mom? I gotta go."

"You're still my favorite daughter." Sensing Amy's impatience, Alex paused only a millisecond longer. "And honey," she said, "try to be patient with all this, okay?"

"Okay," Amy said. "Love you. Bye!"

Alex held the receiver to her cheek. Her face fell to her chest and tears spilled onto her Arizona sweatshirt.

She walked into Lily's study, now rearranged to accommodate her arrival, and picked up the photo of Andy and Amy posing at the summit of Mt. Tom, grinning back at her without a care in the world. The photo was taken a few months before they learned their mother had lung cancer, before their family fell apart, before all hell broke loose.

"Help me God," Alex said. "Please help me with this."

An hour later Lily, holding two bags of groceries, found Alex red-eyed and sorrowful in the kitchen. She put the bags on the counter and put her arms around Alex.

"It's the kids, Lily," Alex said.

Lily held her. "I know, honey," she said, "I know."

41

Before Alex found her way to Lily's house, she had completed five of the six chemo cycles. She was still sick, but less so, and she had begun to visualize the cancer cells packing up and moving on.

The first week of chemo was worse than any flu she'd ever had. She was constantly lightheaded and nauseous, this exceeded by the continuous vomiting and the surprising and severe pain that ran through her nerve endings. She moved miserably from bed to couch to chair, not yet immobilized by the indescribable fatigue she would experience in the days ahead. Mike, Paula, and sometimes her friend Liz stayed with her at all times that week. The kids came and went, doing their best to preserve their eroding teenage normalcy by ignoring their mother when they could. For her part, Alex tried to keep some of her own normalcy within reach and full terror at bay, but the whole scene was unreal.

The second week was more of the same, except by now her nerve pain had traveled to her bones. She was weak, ill, and totally bereft.

"An alien has possessed my body," she said with dripped disgust. "And he has zero zilch compassion."

By the third week of the first cycle, finally, things began to settle down, which is to say that Alex was able to sit at the breakfast table for short stints and laugh at Mike's attempts to make apple pancakes. Even then, preparation for the second round of chemo had already begun, a routine she would come to know intimately.

It was early in the second cycle that Alex lost her hair. With her scalp burning as if she had been scalded, she stood at the bathroom mirror and watched her hair fall into her hands and onto the floor in large chunks. Even her underpants were filled with her pubic hair–"the final degradation," Alex snickered with utter disgust, first to herself, then to Mike, and then to Paula and all of her friends.

"My fucking pubic hair," she said. "Is nothing sacred?"

"Paula," she announced, "I'm shaving every fricking strand of hair I have before it all falls out itself. I'm being pro-active." She used Mike's electric shaver and afterwards opened her jewelry box and put on a pair of wide hoop earrings. She thought about a wig for less than a day before she decided she would let her white, pasty bald, hooped appearance defy her increasingly expanding inner defeat.

By the third week, her skin was flaked, her eyes were dry, her bone pain was treacherously deep, and her fatigue was indescribable. She endured this pattern for five more times over four months. At the end of the fourth cycle Alex told Mike what she could no longer suppress, and at the end of the fifth cycle she pulled out her special linen stationary. Seven years after their last words, in a swirling wild handwriting, she wrote and then mailed a four page letter to Lily Peterson.

42

The aisles at Trader Joe's have an altogether different feel in early spring. It's as though you could pick up a six pack of prepared optimism just as easily as a pizza or an avocado four pack. The ground in Western Massachusetts has been a deepening shade of white all winter and the measured hope of new growth and green grass is not lost on the shoppers of Trader Joe's.

It is Saturday morning and Lily is making her way from the bread section, where she has stocked up on four packages of blueberry scones and one nutty loaf of Milton's Multigrain bread, toward the abundant frozen foods section, where she knows she will find any number of fresh and easy to prepare entrees for the nights when both she and Alex don't or won't cook.

Lily is looking at her grocery list when she turns the corner. She does not see Max until they are within twelve feet of each other. She does not have time to recognize her ambivalence: she has not seen this woman who rescued and loved her since she received Alex's first letter, and for that reason alone she is unprepared to face her now. She is embarrassed, almost ashamed, that she had not made contact before now, has not explained things to her. And yet, despite all that, she is both delighted and relieved to see her again.

Max saw her first. Lily could tell that she had some extra seconds to brace and prepare.

"Hello Lily," Max smiled. She barely paused before she reached out and hugged her. It was a warm gracious gesture and it reminded Lily that Max had single-handedly pulled her up from depression and despair.

"Max," Lily said. "Oh God, you look great."

She could see that Max would once again make this easy for them both.

"I heard Alex is doing well," she said. "I'm so glad."

Lily wanted to freely slide into this transition, but her conscience could not allow it. She had waited too long already.

"Max, do I owe you an explanation?" she asked.

"No Lily. That's ancient history. I've recovered. I had to replace you of course, which was no small feat," Max smiled, "but I'm in a good relationship and I'm glad for you. You must be overjoyed."

"I am overjoyed, Max. We're going on two years that she's been well. Even the kids have come around some. And we're planning a trip to Paris, a kind of celebration."

Max smiled again. She steadied her chin and blinked twice.

"It's great to see you, girl. Take care, okay?"

Lily hesitated. "Max, how would you feel about getting together sometime, for coffee or something?"

The movement in Max's right eye was barely noticeable, but Lily saw it. She had made a mistake.

"No Lily, not now. Maybe someday, okay?"

"Sure," Lily replied. "Great to see you."

With that, Max pushed her cart past Lily's. Moments later Lily looked for her at the checkout counter, and then in the parking lot, but she did not see Max again.

There are special people in life who open doors for you and allow stillness and substance to stroll right through. And sometimes those special people don't cross the threshold with you, sometimes by choice and sometimes by chance. Max and Lily would never rescue dogs together, would never comfort one another when the sky turned black, but as Lily turned onto Russell Street, she knew that Max, even though she would never know, would be with her in spirit through all the good times. Max had saved her life, and this assured her a permanent place in Lily's wildly expansive heart.

43

Clad in apple green velvet sweat pants and a *Life is Good* orange tee-shirt, Alex is jumping up and down in the driveway as Lily pulls in. In three high hops she is leaning into the Mazda's driver's door, wildly swinging her arms, something in her hand fluttering back and forth.

"Tickets for Paris! Here they are, Lily!" Alex screeches. "We're booked!" She flaps the tickets in mid air in front of Lily's ear so she can hear the swishing sound of gleeful anticipation.

"I have groceries…" Lily begins.

"Screw the groceries, Lily! You have to look at these tickets. Right this minute! We're going!"

Lily steps out of the car and snatches the packet from Alex, who is bungy jumping in front of her. She sits down on the little wooden bench Mr. Perry from Truro made for her, and she spreads the perforated papers on her lap.

"Oh wow, Alex, you booked the Hotel St. Germain!"

Alex takes hold of Lily's hands and pulls her up so they are facing one another. She begins to jump up and down and Lily has little choice but to jump with her. She savors the image in front of her—her fiery still buzz cropped five foot four and a half petite fit looking partner whose puzzle pieces have miraculously fit tightly into her own.

"And not just that..." Alex is saying, but Lily has stopped listening. She is looking up at the robin egg blue sky with its soft puff clouds and whispering *'Thank you God, thank you thank you thank you.'*

44

"I've made a deposit on a cemetery plot," this declaration from Alex rolls out just as Lily bites into a stuffed mushroom. Her relaxed dinner at the Apollo Grill is history.

"Alex…" Lily gasps.

Alex sees the panic on Lily's face and realizes that in this lovely moment she has forgotten the precipitous edge they live on, even after a full year of remission.

"No, no Lily, nothing's wrong," she says. "I saw this flyer, a sale on oversized waterfront plots at the Mount Auburn cemetery and I thought, 'what the hell, why not check it out?' One less thing to do now or thirty years from now, and there's room for the kids and even Mike if he wants, and your family."

Alex watches Lily's face relax. She knows that Lily, who prefers to keep herself on an even keel, is often thrown by her constant unpredictability. Still, they both seem to enjoy the steady stream of new ideas that she rolls out, and they both love that Lily supports Alex through most of them.

"Waterfront, huh," Lily says. "So we'll have a water view from the other side?"

"No honey girl," Alex responds, "I don't think it works that way Lily. People who visit us will have a water view, but you and me, we'll have a *heavenly view*. I'm not sure what that includes but for sure it's still you and me still together."

Lily twirls a mushroom around her plate. "Did you ever think it could be this good?" she asks.

"No," Alex answers.

"Do you think we'll ever get used to the blood tests and checkups?"

"No," Alex says. "but Lily, it's been eighteen months. Okay, so I have to pace my breathing and baby my back sometimes. Big deal. And can you believe Andy is on his way to NYU? And your book is coming out this year. And Mike has a girlfriend. We've lucked out, Lily."

Alex reaches across the table and folds Lily's hands into her own. "Lily, the thought of dying and leaving you is unbearable. I can't imagine you without me."

"I can't either, Alex." Lily has lost her fight with composure and a single tear rolls down her cheek.

"Then let's not imagine it. Let's finish our stuffed mushrooms, enjoy our pistachio crusted salmon, and order chocolate flan and two French roast coffees." Alex smiles. "Then let's go home and frolic."

"With the light on or off?" Lily asks.

"On," Alex says emphatically, "The light stays on…"

45

Alex dialed the number with measured nonchalance. She grinned when after a customary two and a half rings, she heard Mike's gruffy voice.

"Hello, Mike Fournier here."

She grinned again. "I heard you're giving Rebecca a ring."

"No comment."

"I'm glad, Mike."

"No comment."

"So maybe now you'll come here for dinner?"

"No."

"I'll make spaghetti and meatballs."

"No."

"Then for my birthday party?"

"No no no."

"Come on Mike. It's time. You know it is."

"I'll decide when it's time, Missy. That part's totally one hundred percent up to me."

"Mike."

"What?"

"I love you."

"Yeah yeah yeah."

"And Mike."

"What?"

"I don't approve of how you reorganized the garage."

"Tough. Organize your own garage."

"Mike."

"What?"

"Don'tcha think we can be in the same room again?"

"Maybe. I'll let you know."

"Mike."

"*What* Alex?"

"Love multiplies, you know."

"Yeah... maybe...bye!"

"Bye back," Alex said. She waited to hang up until she heard Mike put the phone back on its receiver. Then, still smiling, she stood in place so she would remember this moment. The impossible and improbable had happened and they both knew it. Mike and Alex, two star struck kids who married each other two decades ago, two caring parents to two wonderful children, would love one another again. Their relationship would be different, but the love they had pledged to each other when they were barely adults had found its way back to open air and it was reaching for the sun.

46

With three weeks to go before their celebratory return to Paris, Alex is wrestling with the plastic containers that Lily piles one atop another. She steadies the plate of leftover pot roast in front of her and reaches into the cabinet above the stove, feeling around for the six inch circular bowl with the blue rubber top. As she locates it, two other pieces fly out–one bouncing directly off her head and the other unceremoniously falling to the floor, where it defiantly rolls toward the refrigerator.

"Lily!" Alex yells, "I'm not cooking another meal in this kitchen until you clean up the g.d. containers."

Lily appears at the kitchen doorway. She is fresh from the shower, dressed in her favorite black velour sweat suit, a towel wrapped securely around her auburn hair. Alex thinks that she looks debonair.

"You have no appreciation for the fact that half of my beloved dishes and stemware are languishing in storage so we could fit your fiesta ware and martini glasses in my modest kitchen."

Alex feigns surprise. "Honey girl, how could you expect me to co-habitate with you without my martini glasses? Let's be real."

The phone rings just as Lily's long stemmed fingers reach the back of Alex's neck.

"Hold on, hold on," she teases as she swings backwards and grabs the phone.

"Hello."

"Hello. This is Dr. Chambliss."

There are molecular events in life when the slightest word or sound or movement occurs and you know then and there you will never forget who you were the moment before and who you became the moment after.

Alex looks up to see Lily freeze and then bring her hand to her mouth like one of those circus Mime performers. She hears her say, 'This is Lily, Dr. Chambliss.'

When she sees the ashen color on Lily's face, she does not need to hear Dr. Chambliss' response. "I know, Lily, he says. "How are you? I'm afraid I have bad news."

47

Dr. Chambliss arranged to see Alex the following day. Consistent with the dark emotional storm hanging over their household, Lily entered the kitchen dressed in black tencel pants, a black silk blouse, and small sterling silver hooped ear rings. She walked tentatively to where Alex was unloading the dishwasher.

"I'll pick you up at one," she said, resting her hands on Alex's shoulders.

"No Lily," Alex said, "Meet me at the medical center. You can't miss your own award ceremony. After all, to be chosen 'best teacher' two years in a row," Alex looked at her plaintively, "You have to go. I'll drive in with Mike. That way I can stop by the house afterwards and see how the kids are doing. We can meet there and maybe go out for dinner afterwards. Okay?"

The nonchalance in Alex's voice was chilling.

It is the day that Alex and Lily and Mike will meet with Dr. Chambliss to hear news that cannot be good.

"Lily," Alex was again emptying the dishwasher and looked up. "Try to appreciate your award. And stay dry. Bring your umbrella. The weather forecast is nasty."

Lily turned and faced Alex. Their eyes locked on each other for a time so brief no one but the two of them would have noticed.

"Jesus Alex," Lily said.

Alex pulled a small speck of Sebastian style mud from Lily's hair. She forced a smile. "I know it's hard, honey girl, but we still have to show up."

Lily opened the garage door and wondered what their life would look like in three hours. She had clearly understood the tone of Dr. Chambliss' voice on the phone and she dreaded the meeting. In three hours he would be telling them what additional treatment Alex would need, along with his best guess for her survival. Lily had done the research. She understood that Alex could die, that maybe they would bargain out six months, perhaps not even three. Alex had made her intentions clear months ago, matter-of-factly announcing to Lily and her family one night at the Cheesecake Factory that if the cancer ever came back and the outlook was grim, she would not agree to any clinical trials or prolonged care.

"I'm dying with a full head of hair," she had said, "and maybe even new earrings."

In a circular booth with a red patterned fabric, under glitzy amber lights that were probably hand blown Italian glass, Amy had put down her fork. "Mom, you're so morbid. It's not even funny." Her voice shook just enough to underscore the willpower her mother's recurrence would demand of her.

"No honey, I know it's not funny, but there's no reason I have to be bald because of it."

A few renegade tears found their way to Amy's upper lip. She licked them away before she picked up the oversized cloth napkin in front of her and wiped her face. As Alex wrapped her arms around her, she shook her head and forced a smile. This was her mother and no one else, her mother once again lightly reaching into her one-of-a-kind bag of tricks to surround the people she loves in the best way she knows how.

"And Amy," Alex added, picking up her daughter's fork and passing it back to her, "just so you know, I may also want a tattoo."

48

Lily, Alex and Mike stepped into the elevator single file. Mike pushed the button for the lower level, using his Marine training to keep his head erect. When G2 flashed on the numbering system above them, the doors opened and they entered a small foyer that opened to a poorly lit garage with drab cement walls and low ceilings. Mike thought about reaching for Alex's arm but held back when he saw that Lily had securely wrapped her left arm around Alex's right, holding her up and moving her forward. He could not remember seeing his feisty wife so small and fragile, and for a moment he was startled by her willingness to fold into Lily and let herself be carried.

"I'll meet you at the house at five," Lily said. She kissed Alex on her forehead and turned to Mike. "If you and the kids want to have dinner with us, you know you're welcome." She quickly looked at Alex to confirm she had not overstepped her bounds, then she added, "Thanks for being here, Mike."

"Sure," he said. His eyes were moist. Even as Lily kissed Alex and then wrapped her arms around her, he was moving toward his ex-wife. Lily watched them walking arm in arm toward Mike's Lexus, glad for at least that.

Lily reached aimlessly into the turquoise leather bag Alex had given her for Christmas and found her car keys by her customary feel and touch, failing to notice anything around her except the giant circle of loss that would now take up residence and envelope her. For almost two years she and Alex had lived the life she hadn't dared imagine. They were partners, lovers, best friends, soul mates, cohorts, roommates, fellow travelers. Implausibly, the puncturing of the innocent people who suffered because they could not bear to be apart had in some granular way been repaired. Mike was engaged to a ditsy woman named Rebecca Mosley who claimed to make fifty-two variations of Betty Crocker casseroles and adored him. Andy, a tall willowy boy with glistening eyes and an honest handshake, was a junior in college. And Amy, feisty like her mother and just back from a volunteer stint with

City Year, was still eager for her mother's help in choosing colleges and understanding the mysterious world of men.

And Alex, wacky wild wonderful Alex. Lily could not imagine life without her.

"Being with you is like coming home and slipping into your most comfortable shoes and your favorite pajamas all at the same time," Alex had teased her one lazy Saturday morning when they stayed in bed until noon.

Lily had nodded. "Yes, that's exactly true."

And now, on a hostile day with ornery skies and slamming rain, Lily opened her car door, fastened her seatbelt, turned on the engine, and began to cry. She was assaulted by a certain loneliness she had not felt since she watched her mother blowing her a kiss from across the room and forcing a final wave before leaving her in that kindergarten class room. She would be alone like that again, she thought, but this time she would not be distracted. She would not adjust. She did not want to adjust. Life without Alex was unthinkable. Lily Peterson had a strong constitution and she knew how to recover, but she also understood basic astronomy.

When stars cease to burn, their light does not replenish.

49

Lily pulls her parking ticket from the visor and hands it and a ten dollar bill to a Hispanic attendant who is listening to James Brown on a small transistor radio. She merges onto Bay State Road and is jolted by the ferociousness of the rain and the volume and messiness of the traffic. The change in energy is so dramatic she can feel her internal gears shift as she details what has just occurred. What could, should she do to protect Alex, to care for her? What will she need? How can she ever let her go, even when the time for that will be the most loving thing she may ever do?

Lily cannot force herself back to work today. She will meet Alex in a couple of hours and, perhaps with Mike and the kids, they will then begin this new life. *I meet my shadow in the deepening shade,* Lily thinks, a line from Theodore Roethke, which she now fully understands.

The news was grim. Probably three months. Maybe less. She recalls Dr. Chambliss' words and facial expression not even an hour ago.

"I agree with you, Alex," he said. "I don't advise you to travel, but now is the time to do whatever is important to you."

"How long will I feel kinda well?" Alex's tone was fresh and frightened and Lily recognized the charming magical thinking that often accompanied her way of moving in the world.

Slowly Dr. Chambliss had raised his hand and rested it on his glasses. He had obviously been in this situation many times but still, he seemed to steady himself before answering. He cleared his throat.

"One, maybe two months," he said softly.

Lily turns right onto Montclair Avenue and proceeds to the intersection of Montclair and Cormorant. She is irritated by the relentless sound of her windshield wipers on high speed, and even then she can barely see ten feet in front of her. She does not see the Chevy Impala that has raced through the red light until it slams into her with such force that she is thrown against the steering wheel and partially through the windshield. Covered by broken shards of glass that seem to penetrate her skin from all angles, she instinctively raises her hand to her face, glad she is outside and can see the sky, her eyes open, lost somewhere she does not know, dimly thankful for the cold rain that counteracts the raging heat within her. She is wedged between her seat and the dashboard, her seatbelt clasped in place. She hears a distant siren grow louder, until it is replaced by a human voice very close to her.

A college aged kid with curly brown hair and a turned up nose begins talking to her. "It's okay, ma'am," he says nervously, "we'll help you."

As the police begin to rope off the area, an older man with a buzz cut and an authoritative voice has crawled onto the crumbled hood of Lily's car and can see that her body is wedged inside in a way that she cannot be freed without cutting through the driver's door. He clears as much broken glass as he can around Lily's head and face and tries to reach inside to unbuckle her seatbelt. He cannot reach the clasp without the risk of moving her, and he will not do that.

He puts his face near Lily's and whispers to her, "It's alright, honey, don't worry." He rests his fingers on her neck and takes her pulse. Outside, the Jaws of Life begins slicing through the driver's door. Lily hears a grinding sound as the Impala is being pulled away from the Mazda's door, its steel so mangled it looks like it was never there to begin with.

A teenage boy, perhaps seventeen wearing ripped jeans and an Abercrombie and Fitch tee shirt stands to the side, crying and repeating, "I didn't see her. The rain was too bad. Oh God Jesus, I just got this car. My parents will kill me....it's my graduation present." A police officer stands by the boy until a second ambulance arrives and he is reluctantly strapped on a gurney and taken away.

"Tell her family I didn't mean it," he cries before the ambulance doors close. "Tell them I hope she's okay."

It takes six minutes to extract Lily from the cab. With exaggerated precision she is placed and strapped onto a backboard, then slid into the back of the ambulance. Inside, the older man takes her pulse again, tips back her chin, intubates, and puts in an IV line.

"Marty," he motions to the kid with the curly hair, "tell them we're coming in."

Marty picks up the phone and brings it to his lips. "Motor vehicle accident at Cormorant and Montclair," he says. "Driver through the windshield. Appears to be multiple fractures and severe closed head injury. Pulse is weak but present. We're intubating and heading in."

Lily cannot not move. Her eyes widen. She is confused, confined, unsure why her blood feels so hot, why she is free falling, trying to remember where she is supposed to be right now. She moves her lips but no sound comes out. She tries again. "Alex," she finally forces. "Alex Alex."

50

Alex is at the kitchen sink of the Fournier house, washing her hands when the phone rings. Mike waits until the third ring before he picks up the receiver. He is perplexed that the caller asks for his now ex-wife, who has not lived there for almost two years.

"Who's this?" he asks.

"This is Memorial Hospital."

Mike's mind shuffles through a library of possibilities. What could the hospital possibly have to add to the horrific news they have already heard today?

"What's it about?" Mike asks instinctively. He is not going to let Alex get sideswiped.

"It's about Lily Peterson, sir."

Alex looks at Mike. She stops peeling the Gala apple in front of her and freezes, a laser reaction to the perplexity on her husband's face.

"Is this a routine call?" he asks.

"No sir, there's been an accident."

"What? What? Is it about Andy?" Alex screams, her eyes riveted to Mike's face. She sees his head snap back, as if he's been punched.

"It's about Lily, some kind of accident," he says reluctantly, and hands her the phone.

For the second time today Mike is holding Alex up. She has scribbled a note to the kids, who will soon be home from school braced for a report from their mother's doctor that they already know may be bad news. *Lily's had an accident,* Alex writes. *Not to worry. Dad is with me. We'll call soon.*

51

Alex can see Lily from the nurse's station. The trauma
intensive care unit is circular and unless the curtains are
pulled from one end to the other, the pods are wide open.
Lily is lying on a no frills hospital bed in a corner pod
crammed with flashing lights and plastic tubes.

"Oh please," she pleads. "Please. I'm Alex Fournier,
Lily Peterson's partner. Where is her doctor? Can I see
her now?"

A scruffy looking man who resembles the actor
Matt Damon looks up from the computer station and
approaches her. "I'm Dr. DeStefano," he says, extending
his hand to Alex. She holds onto it and does not let go,
even as he directs her and Mike to a corner spot away

from the nurse's station, as if to garner privacy that isn't there. He begins slowly, "Ms. Peterson's head hit the windshield with great force. She sustained multiple fractures and internal injuries but unfortunately, the most serious damage is that she sustained a severe head injury." He says this quickly, as if the speed of information will lessen the impact. "She is unconscious and on a ventilator. That's keeping her breathing," he explains, "but there is no brain activity, no neurological signs. I'm afraid we aren't able to save her."

Alex gasps, then chokes. She pushes her words through uneven breaths. "No, no, no. No, doctor," she cries, "It's me who can't be saved, not Lily. You can't be right. Please, let me see her. She needs me." Alex is leaning against the pale blue trauma wall, upright only because Mike is holding her.

"I'm so sorry," the doctor says. "She's not responding. There is no brain activity." Then, as if he's just understood the tragedy imbedded in his words, he stops and squeezes Alex's hand. "Of course you can go in now," he says. "Take all the time you need."

Lily is lying on her back, covered by a white sheet folded in half, tucked in just below her chin. A one inch plastic tube has been taped to her face and inserted in her mouth. She is attached to a ventilator and a cardiac monitor that makes slow waves like a mountain range and small beeps like a toy truck. Alex finds her hand, will not let go of it. She looks at Lily's swollen face, *that's the way she sleeps,* she says out loud, *that serene look on her face.* She leans forward and positions herself so that her face is touching Lily's ear. "Lily," she whispers, her mouth so close she wants to enter Lily, talk to her from the inside out. "Honey girl, I'm here. It's alright, honey girl. I'm here…I love you Lily. I'm here."

Alex imagines that Lily turns her head, opens her eyes before she shuts them again. She can see that Lily wants to smile, wants to remind her they can get through anything together. She is sure Lily wants to speak.

"Don't try to talk, Lily," Alex says.

Lily does not move but Alex sees past that, watching her force her mouth open, pushing mightily to part her lips.

"Light…on," Alex hears Lily whisper.

The last seconds of life take place in various forms. Sometimes death is a gasping fight for air; other times, it is a deep and peaceful shutting down of the body and its systems, an acceptance to travel inward, and away.

Alex is cradling Lily's face with both hands, breathing for her. The doctors have had their say and the breathing tube has been removed. Alex can feel the warm rain of Lily's smile, the tender movement of her two deep breaths, just before she sighs, and slips away. And then, Lily will be gone, taking with her all the love she had ever hoped for.

"As a parting swan song to the universe, most massive stars explode in a tremendous burst of light and energy when they die. But astronomers have detected a new class of enigmatic stars that appear to fade away quietly, and in the dark.[1]"

It was in this way that Lily Catherine Peterson, age 45, partner to Alex Louise Fournier, stepmother to Andrew John and Amy Elizabeth Fournier, daughter of Paul and Laura Peterson, loving friend and colleague to many, Professor of English Literature at Amherst College, following an automobile accident, passed away at Memorial Hospital on Monday April 30th, in the loving presence of her lifelong partner, and with universal protection and fulfilled abundance provided by her almighty God.

1. Ken Than, *Live Science.* December 20, 2006

52

Dear Lily,

Honey girl, you won't believe this. The last time I wrote you a serious letter I prayed we would be able to find our way back to one another. And we did. Beyond our wildest dreams. Living with you has been one of the deepest joys in my life.

Even before we got this last bit of terrible news about my cancer, I worried so much about how you would do if ever I died. I never for a minute thought that it would be me facing life without you. I think you decided you did not want me to arrive up there by myself, so you went ahead of me to put things in place. I'll tell you this, Lily, whatever fear I have of dying, whatever heartbreak and anger I have leaving my beloved Andy and Amy, Mike and my family, my friends, even the dogs—all of that is lessened now because I know I will at least be back with you. That takes so much of the sting out of the way things have turned out. I can't say for sure how I will feel when I'm too sick to live any longer, but I hope I will at least be relieved to see your smiling beautiful face again.

I love you Lily Peterson. Keep the light on for me.

Love forever,

Alex

53

They are buried on a small hill overlooking the Connecticut River. Theirs is a triple plot, with room for Mike and his second wife Rebecca, for Amy and Andy and their future families, if they choose, and for Lily's parents.

The rose granite headstone is embossed with veranda lettering and an etched outline of a single zinnia, Lily's favorite. Despite the weather or time of year, most visitors say they notice almost immediately a subtle glow around the stone itself.

ALEX LOUISE FOURNIER

1964–2008

LILY CATHERINE PETERSON

1963–2008

'THE LIGHT STAYS ON'

Epilogue

He is tall with his mother's smile. His long fingers are nonchalantly wrapped around the steering wheel, guiding his ten year old Cadillac through the maze of Soho and Washington Square.

"Did you get a card from Mom?" Amy asks her brother. In less than two hours he will graduate from NYU, where he has majored in English and will go on to become a top notch journalist for the *Providence Journal*.

"Yes," Andy says. "It's in the glove compartment."

Amy pulls out a large pink envelope with circular cursive handwriting.

"It's Mom all right," she laughs. She is careful to handle the card inside with a certain reverence.

A cartoon illustration on the outer card shows a young man with wild hair and black glasses and purple high top sneakers and a sweatshirt with the phrase *World U* written in Roman letters. Above the goofy guy, the card says *'To a Wonderful Son on His Graduation from College'*.

Inside Alex has written, *'Woo Hoo! Yay! Finally! Andy, I am SO proud of you. Love Forever, Mom'*. On the left inside flap, in controlled calligraphy print, she has added her own version of being present:

Son, don't ever forget:

1. *Find your passion and use it to do good in the world*
2. *Hold out until you find someone who adores you and who you adore back*
3. *Don't be afraid to make mistakes–it's the best way to learn*
4. *Stay close to your sister and Dad*
5. *You know where to find me   xoxo*

Amy turns away so her tears do not damage the card.

"Hey, lighten up," Andy chuckles. "We should be used to this by now."

Amy returns her brother's grin. "Man, Andy," she says, "sometimes it's like she's still right here."

Andy nods, "Except all those moments when you want like hell to see her and she's not..." He pauses. "Sometimes I hear her voice, Amy, from nowhere."

"Like when?" Amy asks.

"Like once I heard her say 'Andy!' You know, in that tone she used when she wanted to get your attention right away. I'd been drinking and I was groggy driving the car. She startled me awake, really. And once time I swear she smiled at me in my sleep, not like a dream but more like she was right there with me, that goofy grin she has, like she was telling me, 'I'm still here son and it's all fine.'"

Amy puts the card back in the glove compartment. "I wish she'd visit me," she sighs. "These cards...Aunt Paula said there's a supply all the way to our retirement. And remember Lily telling us that the more she did, the more elaborate they became. She said to be prepared for either a song and dance or the equivalent of small explosives from some of the cards."

Andy looks at his sister. His demeanor is solemn. "I'm glad we worked it out with Mom and Lily," he says quietly.

Amy nods. "Me too."

Andy makes a sudden right turn, doing his best to follow the NYU signs that should lead him to the designated parking lot. He wonders if his father will be able to follow the directions. Amy's voice pulls him back.

"And Lily really loved Mom. Do you remember the surprise party she threw for Mom's birthday? Mom was so happy..."

"I always liked how they did little things like that for each other. Remember when Mom arranged for them to try out for *Wheel of Fortune?* How funny was that? What a blast it would have been to see the two of them buying vowels from Vanna!"

Amy locks into her brother's eyes. "Lily was good to us, Andy. She never stood in the way and she put up with all our crap. I think even Dad came to appreciate her." She takes a deep breath. "When Mom died...the last few weeks were so tough, but I kept thinking at least she knew Lily would be waiting for her."

Andy nodded. "At the funeral even Dad said that." Andy wonders how his father will look at his graduation. Mike had called him to ask if he minded if he wore the suit he bought for Alex's funeral.

"Dad," Andy had said, "I don't care what you wear."

Mike had responded softly, "Yeah, I just didn't want to creep you out on such an important day."

Andy turns to his sister. "Oh Dad," he laughs. "That's a whole other story. How many toasts do you think Rebecca will make today before Dad finally tells her to sit down?"

Amy giggles. "She loves those speeches, doesn't she? I think Dad kind of enjoys her ditziness."

"I'm happy Dad's happy," Andy says. He looks at the grin on his sister's face.

"What's so funny?" he asks.

"You won't believe what just came to me. I thought, 'Rebecca is no Lily, but she's okay'. Did you ever think we'd be using Lily as a yardstick?"

Andy shakes his head. "I never saw Mom so damn happy, Amy. She just glowed. And that's how I see her when I think of her now–just so happy."

"I know...me too," Amy says. "She always made me cry when she told us she'll be watching us from the sky to make sure we don't settle."

"Oh jeez," Andy says. "That damn story about being the brightest star in the sky. She scared the bejesus out of me when she first said it."

Amy is quiet again. "Yeah, but do you?"

"Do I what?" Andy asks.

"Do you look for her at night?"

"Shit, yes, I do."

"Me too." Amy stares at her brother.

He continues. "And you know what Amy? I find her sometimes, and I talk to her."

"Me too, Andy. I–"

Beep! Beep! The high pitched sound startles them and they both jump. A red BMW pulls beside the Cadillac. From the front passenger window, there is a blur of bouncing pearls and the color fuchsia. Rebecca is leaning out and waving both hands.

"Yoo hoo. Andy. Hello Amy. Congratulations!"

"Oh Jeez," Amy laughs. "Hello Rebecca and Dad," she yells back with mock exasperation.

They have arrived in the parking lot. As Andy parks the car, his father and Rebecca pull in beside him. He turns to his sister. "Amy, don't mention Mom or the card at dinner, okay?"

"But what if it's the only way we can get Rebecca to stop talking?"

"Well, maybe then," he smiles. "But only if we're desperate, okay?"

"Okay, bro," Amy says. She offers her hand palm up in front of him. He raises his own and they finish off their customary handshake.

"Mom did a good job," he says to her.

"Yup," Amy responds. "Mom did the best."

Printed in the United States
207849BV00001B/1-168/P